WAX APP

1989

No Exit Press
18 Coleswood Road
Harpenden, Herts AL5 1EQ

British Library Cataloguing in Publication Data

Coe, Tucker, 1933–
    Wax Apple – (No Exit Press Contemporary Crime)
    Rn:Donald E Westlake I. Title
813′.54[F]

ISBN 0 948353 54 6

9 8 7 6 5 4 3 2 1

Printed by William Collins, Glasgow

For the mother
Of the purple
First baseman's mitt

ONE

The conductor came through, calling, 'Kendrick! Kendrick!' I glanced at him, then back out at neat white clapboard houses on quiet streets muffled by heavy trees. In the back yards stood small white clapboard garages with doors that opened out instead of lifting. In one back yard not far from the tracks a group of children had tied a child to a tree and were pretending to set fire to him. He was crying, and they were laughing, and over all was the barking of an excited dog – part German shepherd, he looked – prancing and bouncing around them.

The houses grew a little seedier, older, not so well cared for, and gave way to a row of stores, and then the station slid into the foreground and blocked the view. I got to my feet and took down my suitcase and walked through the nearly empty car to the front as the train rolled interminably to a stop. I was two hours from New York and a hundred million miles from home. I stepped down onto the wooden platform, the only passenger from my car getting off here, and went through the old push-door into the station building.

The ticket window was to my left, and on impulse I went over and asked the man when was the next train back to New York. Without checking anything, he said, 'Four-ten.' It was not yet eleven-thirty.

Would I have gone back if there'd been a train right away? Possibly, I don't know. The house would have been empty, Kate and Bill already gone to Long Island. I would have had a month to myself, Kate wouldn't have had to know I'd stayed home until she herself returned. And of course by then it would have been too late to make me go back to The Midway.

Would that have been better as things turned out? But that's a meaningless question, really. In a life in which nothing matters nothing can be either better or worse.

On the other side of the station four identical taxis in orange and gray stood at the curb. A girl laden with suitcases, tennis racket, hat box, shopping bag and raincoat – probably coming home from college for summer vacation – was serially entering the first cab, so I took the second. There was no meter and no notice about fares.

7

The driver, a stocky man with a bushy red moustache, said, 'Where to?'

I said, 'What are the rates?'

'Depends where you're going.'

The address was on a slip of paper in my shirt pocket, but I didn't need to look at it. 'Twenty-seven North Laurel Avenue.'

He pursed his lips under the moustache, studying me in the rearview mirror, trying to figure out exactly how much the market would bear, and finally said, 'Two dollars.'

'I think that's too much,' I said.

He shrugged elaborately. 'That's standard,' he said.

'It's too much.'

'You could try another cab,' he said.

No one else from the train had wanted a taxi, and the other two were still at the curb behind me. 'All right,' I said, and prepared to struggle myself and my suitcase out onto the sidewalk again.

He barely let me get the door open before saying, peevishly, 'Well, what do *you* think it's worth?'

I had no idea, never having been in Kendrick before in my life, but I couldn't go too far wrong if I halved his price, so I said, 'One dollar.'

He twisted around in the seat to look at me without benefit of mirror. 'I tell you what I'll do,' he said. 'I'll split the difference with you.'

'A dollar and a half,' I said.

'Right.'

'That will include tip,' I said.

'Tip?' He raised an eyebrow, and grinned under his moustache. 'This ain't New York,' he said. 'Shut the door, I'm yours for a buck and a half.'

Our route took us through the narrow congested downtown street, angle parking on both sides, one lane of creeping traffic in each direction. On both sides were the stores, the women's clothing shops trying to look modern in nineteenth-century brick buildings, the appliance stores with their dusty windows full of washing machines, the five-and-tens that could have been switched with those of any other city in the country without anybody noticing a thing.

After downtown, we went through the Negro section, old duplexes with sagging porches and only a dim memory of paint, skinny dusty-looking children running in bunches, even the skinny-trunked trees half stripped of their bark. Among the decayed automobiles rusting in front yards I swear I saw a dark blue Fraser.

This strip was followed by the strip of white-clapboard-white-owner houses I'd already seen another part of from the train, and then we came to a much older and once richer section, large turreted and gabled houses on extremely large plots, tall thin windows facing in all directions. But few of the houses were private homes any longer. A mortician was in this one, seven doctors in that one, a convent in a third.

Twenty-seven North Laurel was one of these mastodons, a huge irregular pile of gray stone, three stories high, full of tall narrow windows and architectural cadenzas, with a wrought-iron fence separating the cracked sidewalk from the neat lawn.

There was no sign indicating this building's present status, but the driver obviously knew what it was, because he gave a surprised grunt and said, 'Oh. I didn't know you meant *that* place.'

'Would the price have gone up?'

'Could be,' he said, looking at me in his mirror again.

I paid him, and he said, 'You're gonna work there, huh?'

That was the wrong image. I said, 'Why do you say that?'

'A loony wouldn't have argued the price.'

'They aren't loonies,' I said. Then I corrected myself: 'We aren't loonies.'

'Maybe *you* aren't,' he said, and faced front, ending the conversation.

I struggled out of the cab, and it drove away. There was a break in the wrought-iron fence at the driveway. I walked up the new-looking blacktop, seeing that it continued on past the side of the house, under the nineteenth-century equivalent of a carport, and on to the rear, where I caught a glimpse of a dark wood multi-car garage of more recent vintage than the house. Past the carport two muscular young men in khakis and T-shirts were washing a green Ford station wagon. They glanced at me, and back at their work. They would be Robert O'Hara and William Merrivale, though I had no way of telling which was which. The dossiers hadn't included photographs.

The entrance was under the carport. I went up three steps to an elaborate wooden door, and rang the bell. I stood there for a minute, and then one of the young men called over from the station wagon, 'Go on in. Office to your right.'

'Thank you,' I said, and pushed open the door, and went in. The house echoed. That was my first impression, and it

9

never subsequently went away. Everywhere in that building, there was the sense of an echo reverberating just around the next corner, down some nearby corridor, up in the angle of some other ceiling. However muffled one's own movements might be, whether by carpet or design, an echo existed, independently and without reference to any cause.

The office was to my right, as the young man had said. I went in and found a girl there, making entries with a ball-point pen on three-by-five cards. She had long straight brown hair, folk-singer style, and wore a white shift and white sandals. I knew her name, too, and many of the details of the breakdown which had made her first suicidal and later catatonic and ultimately had led her here to this building, halfway back to a home that no longer really existed. It was embarrassing somehow to know so much about her without her being aware of my knowledge, as though unknown to her her clothing were gaping open in some disgraceful way. I found it difficult to meet her eye.

She had no trouble meeting mine. She looked at me, her eyes still full of whatever she was entering on the three-by-five cards, and said, 'Yes? May I help you?'

'Mitchell Tobin,' I said. We'd decided it would be easier and just as safe to use my own name. 'I'm the new resident,' I said.

'Oh, yes,' she said. 'I have your forms here someplace.' Her desk was very messy, and she riffled through it with the expertise of someone who always keeps her desk very messy, quickly coming up with a large manila folder. She opened this, withdrew a sheaf of papers held together with a paper clip, and passed three of the papers over to me. 'Would you fill these out, please? You can sit at that desk there. You'll find a pen in the drawer.'

I filled out the forms, putting down the lies and half-truths Doctor Cameron and I had agreed upon, and gave them back to the girl, who glanced at them briefly, had me sign two other pieces of paper, and then got to her feet, saying, 'Let's find somebody to show you to your room.'

'Couldn't I find it for myself?'

'I doubt it,' she said. 'It takes a few days to get your bearings around here. We've talked about making a map and giving everybody a copy, but nobody knows the place well enough to make the map.'

She led the way out of the office and down the hall, which turned and forked with no apparent logic. Ahead of us I could hear a ping-pong ball tap-tapping. The girl stopped at a closed door, opened it, and the tapping suddenly increased in volume. She stuck her head in and called, 'Jerry, you doing anything?'

A muffled response.

'Would you show a new man to his room, please?'

Another muffled response, and the girl turned toward me, smiling, leaving the door ajar. A few seconds later, out came a man I thought at first to be young, but then saw to be quite old. He was short and wiry, dressed in khakis and T-shirt like the boys outside, plus scuffed white sneakers, and his gray hair was cropped so close to his head it would almost pass for blond. He had a pinched face, a sharp nose, and a wide mouth open now in a broad smile, showing teeth so clean and so studiedly natural that they had to be artificial.

The girl said, 'Jerry, this is Mitchell Tobin. Mr. Tobin, Jerry Kanter.'

I acknowledged the greeting, telling Jerry Kanter to call me by my first name, and at the same time thinking how very different he was from the mental image I'd picked up from his dossier. Somehow, multiple murderers should be large and somber men, not short narrow-headed men with cheery smiles.

The girl said to me, 'And I'm Debby Lattimore.'

I was distracted by Jerry Kanter, and nearly said *I know*, which would have been disastrous. I caught myself, and said, 'How do you do?'

Jerry said, 'Where's Mitch go?'

'In Marty's room,' she said. She told me, 'Marty left a few weeks ago.'

'Nice place,' Jerry commented, about the room. 'You ready for a hike?'

'I suppose so,' I said.

'If you need anything,' Debby said, 'I'm usually in the office. Or Doctor Cameron will be there.'

'I suppose I should see him,' I said. It would be a relief to be with someone in whose presence I wouldn't have to lie.

'Oh, he'll be around,' Debby said. 'See you later.' She nodded and smiled, and walked away down the hall.

Jerry said, 'This way,' and I switched my suitcase to the other hand and walked with him. 'You're on the second floor,' he said. 'We'll do the back stairway.'

The back stairway was enclosed, but broad enough for us to go up side by side. Jerry said, 'Where were you?'

My first real test. 'Revo Hill,' I said.

He frowned. 'I don't think I know it.'

'In Connecticut.'

'Oh. I don't think we have anybody from there.'

I knew they didn't. That was why Doctor Cameron had picked it.

The corridor we emerged into on the second floor was long and wide and lined with doors. Dark portraits of bygone admirals hung on the walls between the doors. Jerry led me along labyrinthine corridors, with me walking more slowly than necessary in order to try to memorize the way, and at last he opened a door on our right. 'If you can't find the place the first few times you leave it,' he said, 'just ask somebody. Don't leave a trail of bread crumbs, we've got a mouse problem.'

'I'll remember that,' I said.

'Well, I'll see you,' he said.

'Thank you for being my guide.'

'Any time. You play touch football?'

'A little. Not for a long while.'

'Well, naturally,' he said. I didn't understand for a second, and then I saw I'd been on the implied edge of a disastrous slip. If I'd just been released from Revo Hill Sanitarium, naturally I hadn't played touch football for a while. It shouldn't even have been necessary to say it.

I was beginning to see that living a lie isn't quite as easy as it is made out to be in movies and books. The direct questions can be handled readily enough, but how does one edit his unconscious assumptions?

Jerry didn't notice anything particularly wrong, however. He merely assured me I would have a place on the touch football field whenever I wanted it, and went away, and I went into my new room.

It was quite large, really, and made to seem even larger by being underfurnished. The single bed on the right was far too small for the room, and so was the brown metal bureau on the opposite wall. The imitation Persian carpet was of good size, but the two chairs, writing desk and floor lamp were not by any means enough furniture to place on it.

I put my suitcase down, shut the door, and went over to look out one of my three windows. I saw lawn and trees, and through the leaves and branches I could make out the orange brick of the house next door. This was the opposite side of the building from the carport and Robert O'Hara and William Merrivale, the two young men washing the station wagon.

I unpacked, putting my things away in the closet and bureau, finding no trace of the former resident. The room had been anonymous when I'd walked into it, and when I was done unpacking it was still anonymous, an empty large under-furnished room waiting for somebody other than me.

I didn't want to stay in here any more than necessary, and in any case I should be out and around, getting a look at the place. And I hadn't met any of the injured ones yet. So I left the room, uncomfortable that there was no way to lock the door, and made my way with some difficulty and one wrong turn back to the staircase Jerry and I had come up. I opened the door and stepped through, shut the door behind me, started down the stairs, and felt something catch my ankle.

I tried to stop myself, but there was no banister and my flailing hands bounced off the side walls. My balance was gone. I felt myself toppling, saw the staircase stretching down ahead of me with all those sharp stair edges like the serrations of a steak-knife, and far far away was the bottom.

I should have gone limp, of course, I should have relaxed and fallen like a rag doll, that's the way to minimize the danger of injury, but I wasn't thinking at all. I'd panicked, and I went down with my arms stretched out rigid in front of me, my hands wide open, my fingers splayed out, and when I hit I heard the dry quick snap in my right forearm. And nothing more.

TWO

I dreamed I was working on my wall, and for some reason my arm got caught in it. I looked at it in irritation and dismay and bewilderment, my arm stuck into the wall halfway up to the elbow, cement packed hard all around it, the bricks pressing against it on all sides. I couldn't understand how I'd done it, how I'd trapped my arm in there without noticing. I tried to move it, but the pressure was too great all around, and my straining made a sickening clammy ache travel up my arm and down my side and into my stomach, so I thought I would faint. Instead, I woke up.

My wall was still in my mind, so I didn't make sense for a moment out of what was actually in front of my eyes. In my confusion, all I had to cling to was the thought of my wall.

It's a good wall. I'm building it myself, slowly, carefully, a very little bit at a time. I'm in no hurry to finish it, the construction is its own purpose, and the wall is emerging from the ground straight and solid and permanent. When done it will be two feet thick and ten feet high, enclosing the back yard of my house on three sides, with no openings. The house itself is the fourth side, and when the wall is finished the only way into the back yard will be through the house. I have been working on the wall now for over a year, except during the coldest part of the winter, and it has attained so far a height of just over two feet all the way around. This may seem like slow progress, but to me at times it seems far too fast, because I can see that a day will come when the wall will be finished, and what will I think about then?

I turned my head, my mind full of thoughts about the wall, and gradually I began to recognize elements of the room I was in, and then memory fell into place and I remembered where I was and why I'd come here. And what had happened, the falling, the stairs speeding toward me, the dry snapping sound inside my arm.

My arm. I tried to lift it, and it seemed to be held down with heavy weights. I lifted my head instead, and looked along the length of my arm, and saw a fresh white plaster cast covering it from just below the elbow to the middle of my fingers. And my head – which ached, a dull foggy ache that made me fuzzy-minded – was wrapped in bandages.

So he'd gotten me. On arrival, a greeting from my prey. And I had come here warned against him.

Was he warned against me? Did he know who I was and what I was doing at The Midway? Or was it purely accident that the accident had been arranged for me? That seemed more likely, and in any case I preferred to believe it.

But how badly was I hurt? With my free hand I pressed and poked at my head beneath the bandage. Two areas near the right front responded with sharp pain, but my fingers didn't find anything that seemed really serious. I probably had cuts and bruises up there, that's all.

My arm? Broken, no question of that. And any other injuries?

I found it surprisingly easy to sit up, but the instant I did so a blinding headache swept over me, as though a bucket of liquid pain had been dumped on my head. I sat there with head bowed for half a minute or so, till the pain subsided again, and then took inventory of myself.

I had a bad burn on my right knee. Also a tender spot in my rib cage on the right side. Those two, plus the head and the arm, seemed to be the extent of my injuries.

I was amazed that I didn't feel weaker, but then I saw the small puncture mark on the inside of my left elbow. A doctor had been to see me, of course, the cast on my right arm demonstrated that, and he must have given me something to make me sleep. I'd done a lot of healing already, while unconscious.

What time was it? The floor lamp was lit and there was darkness outside my windows now, meaning it had to be after nine o'clock at night, and it had been barely noon when I'd taken the spill. My watch had been taken off, along with the rest of my clothing, so I could only make guesses.

I was starving. The question about time had made me suddenly stop and realize how hungry I was, and it was my stomach rather than my sense of duty or question about time that drove me to get out of bed.

All movements affected my head, but by moving very slowly and carefully I managed to keep the pain to a low background irritation. I slid my legs over the side – I was dressed in nothing but pajama bottoms – and with a great deal of care stood up.

Ah. I wasn't quite as strong as I'd thought while in the

15

safety of the bed. Standing was another matter. I leaned against the wall beside the bed for a minute, till a certain dizziness passed, and then stepped in slow small movements across the large room to the bureau on the opposite wall, on top of which I could see my watch.

Twenty minutes to five. In the morning? I held the watch to my ear, and it was ticking. I'd been unconscious nearly seventeen hours. No wonder I was so hungry.

I dressed with a great deal of difficulty. Not only did my head wince at every careless movement, I had a lot of trouble getting any useful assistance from the fingers of my right hand. They jutted from the cast, but didn't want to work well. Zipping my trousers was bad enough, but tying my shoelaces was very nearly impossible, and when I finally had loose sloppy knots done on both, the headache was with me full-strength. I sat in the chair at the writing desk a few minutes, till I felt a little better, and then got up to finish dressing.

A shirt was impossible, so what I finally did was put on the tops to the pajama bottoms I'd awakened in, leaving the right sleeve dangling empty and buttoning the buttons awkwardly with my left hand.

I had brought a small pencil flashlight, and this I tucked into my hip pocket before leaving the room. It was quarter past five when at last I opened the hall door, it having taken me over half an hour to get dressed.

The corridor lights were on. I shut the room door behind me and stood listening to the silence a moment. The echo was muted late at night, but it still existed, vibrating far away out of sight, as though some tiny bird were caged in the attic.

I found the staircase this time with no false turns. It was empty, silent, enclosed, with lit ceiling globes at top and bottom. I took out my pencil flash, awkwardly sat down on the top step, switched on the flashlight, and carefully examined the baseboard on both sides. I could see nothing at all on the left, but on the right I could just barely make out the small hole where a nail or tack of some kind had recently been.

So my guess was probably right. He had stretched some sort of wire or string across the top of the stairs, just at ankle height. I distinctly remembered the feeling that something had caught my ankle.

He'd been taking quite a chance this time. He'd set the trap in broad daylight – it hadn't been there when Jerry Kanter and I had come upstairs – and then he'd had to wait nearby until someone was caught, so he could quickly go and remove the evidence, the wire and tacks.

This was his fifth booby trap, and he hadn't yet repeated himself. The first had been a table that had collapsed in the dining room, bruising the legs of the two people sitting there and burning them both with hot coffee. The second was when a resident opened a seldom-used storage closet and a six-foot-long metal piece of bed frame which had been leaning against the door on the inside fell out and hit him in the face, cutting his mouth and chipping two of his teeth. The third was the collapse of a small terrace outside a woman resident's room while she was standing on it to watch a touch football game on the lawn below, the result being that she was now in the local hospital with a broken neck and three broken ribs, among other injuries. And the fourth was a ladder rung that had given way while a resident was doing some work on the gutters, so that he fell and broke his leg.

It was the ladder accident that had tipped his hand, since another resident, in putting the ladder away, had seen that it was partly sawn through, and had taken the evidence to Doctor Cameron. They'd checked the terrace and found that that had been tampered with also. There was no way to prove the bed frame had been left dangerously against the door on purpose, and the collapsed table had long since been thrown out, but the evidence of the third and fourth accidents was enough to force Doctor Cameron to take action. The action he had chosen to take was me. I had agreed with great reluctance to come up here and pretend to be another resident while trying to find out who was causing these injuries, and I had promptly become victim number five.

My only consolation was that so far no one had been victimized twice, though even that was small consolation since most of the booby traps had operated strictly by chance. Anyone at all might have opened that closet door or started down these stairs. Half a dozen residents would have been likely to use that ladder. The injurer didn't seem to care in particular who was hurt, just so someone was.

A small sound made me look up. I was still sitting hunched on the top step, the pencil flashlight beamed at the tiny hole in the baseboard, my useless right arm imprisoned inside my pajama top, and the small sound made my hackles rise. Was I about to be pushed? Could I survive two falls like that in the same day?

17

I saw black tennis shoes, black denim work pants. My right arm wanted to reach out and grasp the wall, the floor, anything at all for protection and support. In order to look up, to see any more of this person, I would have to tilt my head back over the yawning staircase, and I was very reluctant to do so.

A mild voice said, 'Did you lose something?'

My feet were braced against the second and third steps. I looked up, and above the baggy-kneed black work pants, the faded flannel shirt, the open black cardigan sweater, blinked a round, curious, rabbit-mild face. He wore wire-framed spectacles, behind which his eyes were pale and watery. His hands, small and pale and soft, hung at his sides.

I said, 'Yes. I lost' – I cast about for something I might have lost, something small – 'my ring,' I said at last, and held up my bare left hand, the flashlight still held in it. 'I dropped it when I fell,' I said.

'Wouldn't it be at the bottom?' He wasn't suspicious, merely curious. The perfect spectator, friendly and interested and not involved.

'I suppose it would be,' I said. I struggled to my feet – he didn't offer to help me – and went up the two steps to the landing, where I felt safer. I had no idea which of the residents this man might be – after multi-murderer Jerry Kanter had turned out to be a spry little aging teen-ager, I was going to make no more guesses based on dossiers – but whoever he was and however mild his appearance, he was potentially the planter of the booby traps, and I was more than a little nervous in his presence.

I also felt I had to explain myself. I didn't want the residents to begin to suspect there might be something false about me. At the moment, only Doctor Cameron and the resident who'd discovered the sawn-through rung and I knew that the recent rash of accidents was not accidental. I said, 'I woke up and I was very hungry. Then I thought I'd look for my – my ring.'

'I should think it would have been found by someone else by now,' he said. 'Doctor Cameron will have it.'

'No one would take it for himself?'

'Steal it?' He was shocked at the idea. 'Not *here*, not in The Midway! This is not like the outside world, you know.'

'I know,' I said. 'But there's never any petty thievery, none at all?'

'How could there be? You'd have to tell about it in group therapy, and then they'd make you give it back.' He said this

18

as though it was obvious, and I had merely forgotten it. 'Besides,' he added, 'stealing is merely an indication of insecurity, and who would ever feel insecure in The Midway?'

I would, for one, but I didn't say so. But now, seeing the solemn assurance in this little man's eyes, I finally understood Doctor Cameron's passion for secrecy. The Midway was a haven for people recently out of mental institutions who for one reason or another felt unable to go directly into the mainstream of society, which meant these people were delicate and fragile creatures who very much needed the feeling of security The Midway afforded them. If they were to learn that behind every door, within every piece of furniture, somewhere in every room there was a potential injurious booby trap, what would it do to their newly-gained mental stability? Particularly once they were told the perpetrator was necessarily one of them, and that all of them were equally under a cloud of suspicion.

So I didn't disagree with the little man. Instead, I said, 'You're up pretty early yourself, aren't you?'

'Oh, I sleep very little,' he said. 'I was just going down to the kitchen for a snack. May I join you?'

'I wish you would,' I said. 'I have no idea where the kitchen is.'

'Oh, I know this house backwards and forwards,' he said. 'Come along, I'll show you.'

I let him go first, and he stepped carelessly down the stairs, blithe in his belief of The Midway's security. At the bottom I was prepared to stage a little search for my nonexistent ring, but he opened the door without pausing and went on through.

As we walked along the constantly shifting corridors of the first floor, I said, 'By the way, my name is Mitchell Tobin. I just got here today, you know.'

'I know,' he said. 'You came by taxi. I saw you drive up. Tobin, you say?'

'Yes. I'd like you to call me Mitch, if you would.'

'People call me Dewey,' he said. 'It's a sort of nickname.'

'Hello, Dewey,' I said.

He smiled blankly at me, and walked on.

The kitchen was large and old-fashioned, but with fairly new appliances. Doctor Cameron, while describing The Midway to me, had told me something of the place's finances. The people here paid nothing, support coming primarily from a foundation grant, plus a small subsidy under a Federal Health, Education and Welfare program. The foundation owned this house, and leased it to Doctor Cameron — whose brainchild The Midway was — for a dollar a year. These modern appliances would no doubt have been put in by the foundation when it had bought the building for Doctor Cameron seven years ago.

Dewey expressed a wish to cook for both of us, and asked me what I had in mind to eat. It was really too early for breakfast, and yet the hour was even more inappropriate for lunch or dinner. I asked him what he planned to eat and when he said scrambled eggs I said that sounded fine for me also. It did, but there was also the advantage that my food would not be prepared separately from his. There was no reason to suspect Dewey in particular — except that he was prowling around the house at five in the morning — and the accidents had not so far included anything along the lines of food poisoning, but there was something about being in this house, knowing what I knew, surrounded by former mental patients, that was making me cautious almost to the point of paranoia.

While Dewey bustled around the kitchen, obviously enjoying himself, I watched him and tried to figure out which one he could be. None of the residents was named Dewey, nor did any of them have names that would quickly alter into such a nickname. There were three men in particular I thought he might be, having eliminated everyone else simply on the basis of sex or age, but I couldn't seem to narrow it any more than that. And it would surely have seemed a little odd if I pressed the point about his name. I'd find out in time, in any case.

The scrambled eggs were delicious, and so was the coffee. I had to eat left-handed, which I found awkward, and there was no choice but to let Dewey butter my toast, which he diffidently volunteered to do. He was very pleased to have someone to chat with, that was plain, but was hypersensitive to the possibility that he might be forcing his attentions. When talking about The Midway he could be voluble and animated, but other than that he was extremely shy and reticent.

I kept the conversation alive mostly by asking him questions about The Midway, the answers to which I already knew from Doctor Cameron. It was clear that Dewey loved the place, but when I asked him how long he'd been here his answer was vague. I knew the house rules were that no one could stay here more than six months — partly because of the demand for space, but even more in order to avoid having any of the residents become too attached to The Midway and become unable ever to leave — and I wondered how close Dewey was to that

20

cutoff date. I doubted departure would be easy for him when the time came.

The impression I got was that he must be very near the end of his half-year. At one point he said, 'I do like a chance to chat with new people when they first come here. I'm an old settler here, you might say, and I can answer a lot of questions that Doctor Cameron might be too busy for.'

Would a man like Dewey, nearing the end of his six months, become jealous of those who would still be here after he was gone? And would he try to punish them for being where he could no longer be? I had no idea how compelling such a motive might seem to a man like Dewey, which hampered me very badly. The motive almost necessarily had to be an irrational one – the idea of punishment of some kind kept circling in my head – and those are by far the hardest to deduce.

When breakfast was done, Dewey assured me he'd take care of the dishes, and I had no choice but to leave them to him. If I'd had the use of both hands I would have insisted on helping, but as it was there wasn't much useful I could do in a kitchen. He offered to show me the way to the stairs, but I said I preferred to try for them on my own, besides which I was interested in just strolling around the place for a while. When I left, he was starting to wash the dishes. 'See you around,' I said.

'I'll be here,' he said, over his shoulder.

I left the kitchen and strolled a while, following corridors this way and that, occasionally coming to dead ends, but usually finding that corridors led eventually to other corridors. After a while, I saw that the layout was not as complex as it appeared, that there really weren't that many corridors, it was just that they crossed one another so much. This proliferation of junctions had the dual effect of wasting a great deal of interior space and at the same time creating a lot of unnecessary confusion.

I found the front stairs after a while, a broad open staircase with curving banisters. It seemed overly grandiose, not for the house but for its placement. It came down to enter broadside a fairly narrow corridor, with a blank wall facing it on the other side. I frowned over this for a while, and then noticed that this section of wall was slightly different from the wall farther on, mostly in that the baseboard was not quite so tall or complex. The impression I had was that some larger space had originally existed here, and a revamping of the interior had done away with the large space while leaving the heavy staircase that emptied into it. Perhaps there'd originally been a front entrance, later superseded by the present entrance at the side. If so, there should be some indication on the outside, and later on, in daylight, I would look it over.

I continued to stroll around, the corridors all being fully lit, possibly for the reassurance of the residents, and the third time I came to the broad front staircase I decided I'd done the first floor enough for this time, and I went upstairs.

It had been my intention to wander around the second floor as I had wandered around the first, but by the time I reached the head of the stairs I'd changed my mind. I'd been feeling pretty good ever since breakfast, the stroll up and down the corridors not having taxed my strength in any appreciable way, but climbing a flight of stairs quickly reminded me that I was not in the best of physical condition. I reached the second floor winded and dizzy, the headache returning, and a great heavy weariness settling throughout my body. The only sensible thing for me to do right now was go straight back to my room and rest for an hour or so, and I knew it.

Unfortunately, it wasn't quite that easily done. This was the first time I'd come upstairs via the front staircase, and I had no idea where my room was from here. The only thing to do was to start walking and hope that sooner or later I would stumble into familiar territory.

And so I did, after a fairly short walk. A closed door looked familiar, and when I opened it the back staircase was there, just as I'd suspected. From here, I knew my way home, and two minutes later I was safely again in my room, lying down on my bed, very nearly smiling from the pure physical pleasure of relaxation.

Not that I was tired. How could I be tired, after sixteen hours' sleep? It wasn't yet six-thirty. I'd been awake less than two hours. But I was weak, and I could spend this rest period thinking about the people I'd met so far and trying to comprehend the kind of motive that would lead one of the residents of this building to savagely and randomly injure his fellows.

Five minutes later I was asleep.

THREE

I had first met Doctor Fredric Cameron five days before my arrival at The Midway, on Wednesday the eighteenth of June. It was a pleasantly sunny day, not too hot, not yet summer-muggy, and I had worked three leisurely hours on the wall in the morning. Kate first mentioned him during lunch, saying, 'Mitch, there's a man coming to see you this afternoon.'

I looked at her with mistrust. She can't help wanting to push me back among the living, and I have to be always on my guard against her. I said, 'What man?'

'He wants you to do a job for him, Mitch,' she said quickly, before I could make any comment of my own, 'Marty Kengel-berg sent him to you. It's something you could do, and we could use the money.'

Marty Kengelberg is an old friend of mine from the happy days. Twice in the two years since I'd been kicked off the force I'd reluctantly agreed to take on jobs suitable to an ex-cop – an ex-cop who'd been booted out not for dishonesty but for dereliction of duty – taking them mostly because the family needed the money and I don't have a job these days, and since the second one Marty has come around two or three times to suggest that I put in an application downtown for a private detective's license. He doesn't understand that I have left more than the New York Police Department. Kate does, but wants to bring me back.

So here they were together, Marty and Kate, urging some new job on me, Marty out of old friendship and the mistaken idea that I really did want to work, Kate in hopes that some job like this would so distract my mind that a magical cure would take place and all painful paralyzing memories would disappear forever from my brain. It won't happen, of course, partly because that isn't the way minds work, and partly because I really don't feel I have the right not to feel guilty about what I did.

But nevertheless the man was coming. 'He'll be here at two o'clock,' Kate said. 'I promised you'd listen to him, but I told him you might say no.'

'It's a nice day,' I said. 'I was going to work on my wall this afternoon.'

'He won't keep you long,' she promised. 'And he told me something about the problem, Mitch, and it does sound interesting.' She said that so hopefully, looking at me with such open yearning for some sort of lively response from me, that it was impossible to refuse her.

So I saw Doctor Fredric Cameron when he arrived at two o'clock, and when it turned out he was a psychiatrist I felt one instant of rage and betrayal, thinking that there was no real job after all, that Kate had just decided to sneak some psychiatric assistance up on my blind side.

But she hadn't. She wouldn't, not Kate. Doctor Cameron did have a real problem, and any problems of mine didn't interest him.

He wasn't my idea of what a psychiatrist should look like, he had more the look of a well-fed businessman. Gray suit, quiet tie, heavy face, thinning and graying hair, the total effect more that of a Kiwanis Club booster than the founder of a place like The Midway.

'The Midway,' he told me, 'is a halfway house for former mental patients. Do you know anything about the halfway house concept?' I didn't, so he said, 'Halfway houses are places for people returning to society but unable or unwilling to make the plunge all at once. There are halfway houses for ex-drug addicts, former convicts, I understand there's even one in Florida for ex-priests. The concept is that the inhabitants of a halfway house are free to come and go as they please, but are still in a semi-protected environment, and living among other people with similar problems and a shared understanding.' He took a pipe from his side jacket pocket, but didn't light it. He just sat there with his hand cupped around the bowl. 'The idea does work,' he said.

He went on to tell me further details about The Midway, economic and social and psychiatric. It turned out he was the founder and guiding spirit of the place. He was proud of his brainchild, as he probably had every right to be, and it showed. I could see he'd be willing to go on telling me about the place all afternoon, so I finally broke in to ask, 'And what's happening there to cause the trouble?'

He frowned, not liking to be reminded of the snake in his Eden. 'Someone,' he said heavily, 'is injuring our residents.'

I said, 'They're doing what?'

'Causing accidents,' he said, and went on to tell me about the four accidents, the discovery of the sawn-through ladder rung and the corroboration of the tampered-with terrace.

When he was done I asked him if he'd gotten in touch with the local police, and he shook his head, saying, 'No, we did not. We would prefer not to have to, which is why I've come to you.'

'The police would be better,' I said. At that time I still thought there might be a way to avoid this job.

There wasn't. 'The Midway,' Doctor Cameron explained, 'is not in New York. We're in a small town upstate called Kendrick. The local people disapprove of us under the best of circumstances, and the local police are not the best-trained or most modern police officers in the world. Mr. Tobin, the people at The Midway are convalescents, they're walking wounded. Many of them are still only tentatively on the road to health. To be given the rough treatment, the suspicion and open hostility they would be bound to receive at the hands of the local police if I were to report what's going on would be detrimental to all of them, and perhaps critically so for some.'

'As critical as a broken leg?'

'Much more so,' he said. 'Bones knit much more readily than minds.'

There was no answer to that. I said, 'Do they know what's going on?'

'The residents? No, only Bob Gale and myself.' Bob Gale was the young resident who'd discovered the ladder rung and brought it to Doctor Cameron's attention. 'The atmosphere of suspicion and fear I would create if I did tell them,' the doctor said, 'would once again be much worse than the possibility of a broken bone.'

I said, 'You're taking an awful chance, Doctor Cameron.'

'I'm aware of that,' he said. 'That's why I want this situation cleared up just as quickly as possible. Bob Gale brought me the ladder rung the day before yesterday. I've been trying to decide how best to handle the problem, and it seems to me what I need is a professional. Someone who can come to The Midway, move in as though he were simply a new resident, and try to find out who is doing all this.'

'Move in,' I repeated. 'You want me to come live there.'

'For a while, yes,' he said. He didn't seem to be hiding any secondary motives. He said, 'If we're to keep the situation a secret from the residents, there's no other way I can think of to handle it.'

I asked him a few more questions after that, nothing significant, and then told him I would think it over and let him know. He said something about there being some urgency in hearing my answer, and I promised not to think it over too long, and he left.

Kate wanted me to do it, of course, and we both knew her reasons, but she also knew she had to have some different reason if she were going to persuade me, and she was ready. 'Bill and I could go out to Hal's on the Island,' she said. 'You know Bill's been hoping he could get away to the ocean for a while during summer vacation, and I would like it, too. We don't mind staying here, we understand that you don't want to leave the wall, but if you took the job you'd be going up to that place to live for a while and that would give Bill and me a chance for a real summer vacation.'

Sometimes I wish I had the courage to leave entirely. Kate would be a thousand times better off without me, and God knows so would Bill. What does a fifteen-year-old boy need with a father who just broods in the house all the time? It would lighten both their lives if I were simply to pull up stakes and go away, and there are times when I wish I could do it, but I just can't. I'm afraid to go, and that's the truth. If I didn't have Kate, and Bill, and the house, and my wall, if I didn't have these threads of my cocoon to enclose me, I doubt I would long allow me to go on living.

So Kate had chosen the perfect argument. I would be out of their lives for a month, at least.

Doctor Cameron was staying at a hotel in midtown Manhattan. I called him that evening and accepted the job, and we met in his hotel room the next day to begin the groundwork for my impersonation. We decided on a background for me that paralleled my own life without revealing me to be an ex-cop, and Doctor Cameron dictated a letter of application which I wrote and sent off to The Midway. Because the clerical staff there was composed entirely of residents – a cook, Doctor Cameron and one other psychiatrist were the only employees – I had to put in an actual letter of application. The return address was Revo Hill, not only because no one now at The Midway had ever been there, but also because an old friend of Doctor Cameron's was on the staff there and would intercept the reply.

Doctor Cameron also gave me dossiers on the twenty-one people now living at The Midway, plus verbal descriptions of the cook, a local widow named Mrs. Garson, and the other psychiatrist, a younger man named Lorimer Fredericks.

On Saturday, Doctor Cameron returned to Kendrick, and on Monday Kate and Bill went happily off to Long Island while I boarded the train with my suitcase and came up to The Midway, where I promptly became the fifth victim of the man — or woman — I was supposed to catch.

After my induced accident and my nocturnal breakfast with Dewey and subsequent stroll around the first floor, I slept another five hours, waking up just before noon to find that someone had removed my shoes and socks and covered me with a blanket while I slept. And when I got out of bed — being much stronger this time — I found on the bureau a miniature bottle of Ballantine Scotch and a note in printed capital letters, ballpoint pen on ordinary white notepaper, saying:

I'M SORRY IT WAS YOU

The dining room was large and green, with a row of small-paned French windows overlooking trees and green shrubbery at the front corner of the house opposite the driveway. There were half a dozen small tables widely spaced, each neatly set for four people. When I walked in, at about quarter past twelve, two tables were fully occupied and the others were all empty, leaving me no choice but to sit down alone.

At one of the other tables Debby Lattimore, the girl from the office, was sitting with Robert O'Hara and William Merrivale, the two young men who'd been washing the station wagon yesterday. Another young girl completed the foursome and I knew she had to be Kay Prendergast, the only other very young female among the residents. To look at her, painfully slender, mousy in both appearance and manner, her dull brown hair in a puffy style at least fifteen years out of date, it was hard to equate her with the facts in her dossier. Three illegitimate children before her seventeenth birthday, two extended run-away attempts, a long record of shoplifting; her adolescence had been a violent extended scream culminating in her commitment by a court to a state mental institution three months before she was to have graduated from high school. She was now twenty-two, and the five years in the institution had apparently dampened her entirely from what she had once been.

Neither Jerry Kanter nor Dewey, the other two residents I'd already met, were in the room, the other occupied table containing four female faces entirely new to me. The temptation to try to guess which face went with which history was nearly overpowering, but I managed to avoid the bad manners of staring. As did they; no one paid any obvious attention to the fact that the dining room now contained someone eating lunch while wearing a pajama top.

The meal system at The Midway was fairly simple. Breakfast was served between seven and eight-thirty, lunch from twelve to one-thirty, dinner between five-thirty and seven. Mrs. Garson, the cook, prepared one menu, no choices, and a different resident each meal had the job of waiter and kitchen assistant. The waiter for lunch today was a thin fiftyish man with a mournful face and large ears, who reminded me of a Norman Rockwell painting. Fat people in Norman Rockwell paintings look as though they've always been fat and enjoy it, but thin people have extra rolls of flesh, as though they've just recently lost a great deal of weight. They also tend not to look happy about it. This waiter, in a gray business suit and conservative tie under a full-length white apron, with his lined mournful Norman Rockwell face, was a very comical figure until he came close enough to see his eyes. Deep-set and shadowed, they weren't merely mournful, they were despairing. I met his look, and knew at once that he, like me, was impaled forever on one unchangeable instant in the past.

He was bringing me a bowl of chicken noodle soup, and as he put it down he said, 'Well, you're the new fellow, ain't you? Tobin.' His voice was deep and resonant, like that of a radio announcer.

'That's right,' I said. 'Mitch Tobin.'

'Walter Stoddard,' he said. He nodded at my right arm, encased in the pajama top, the sleeve hanging empty. 'Sorry about your accident.'

'I suppose I'll live,' I said. 'If I can eat one-handed.'

'We're having swordfish today,' he said, 'one of Mrs. Garson's specialities. No cutting required.'

'Wonderful,' I said, and he managed a brief mournful smile and went away. I watched him go, knowing the details of what was impaling him, wondering on what scale we could compare – to mix the metaphors – his albatross with mine. Walter Stoddard had murdered his seven-year-old retarded daughter and had then tried to take his own life. He had broken down completely afterward and had just completed his third stay in an asylum. His wife, like my Kate, had never turned away from him. She was waiting now for him to complete his voluntary exile at The Midway and come home to her. It was impossible to be sure why his earlier attempts to rebuild his life had failed, just as it was impossible to be sure why he was so reluctant to go home to his wife this time, but it was possible to make guesses. I had the feeling there might be differences among kinds of forgiving wives, and that I was much more fortunate in Kate than Walter Stoddard was in the woman who had elected to stand by him.

I was nearly done with my soup – it was quite good, but I couldn't get over the oddity of eating it left-handed – when a young man sat down at the place to my right. 'Hello, Mr. Tobin,' he said. 'I'm Bob Gale.'

'How do you do?' He was the one who'd discovered that the ladder had been tampered with. Looking at him, I saw an open-faced young man of about thirty, with nothing in his expression or manner to show that his experiences in Vietnam had driven him to the psychiatric wing of a VA hospital for three years. He seemed now to be simply an open, cheerful, amiable young man, in fact younger than the thirty I knew him to be.

'The question is,' he said, leaning closer to me and talking softly, 'how are you doing?'

'We probably shouldn't look furtive,' I suggested, 'since we're supposed to have just met.'

'Oh.' He sat back, looking confused and guilty, which was no better.

'Here comes your soup,' I said. 'I was hoping to have a talk with you and Doctor Cameron after lunch anyway.'

'Oh, good.' He sat back to let Walter Stoddard put down his soup. 'Chicken noodle? Great.'

'And swordfish,' Stoddard told him. He looked at me. 'Are you ready for yours?'

'I'll wait for Mr. Gale,' I said.

'Bob,' he said. 'Call me Bob.'

Stoddard went away, and I said to Gale, 'I have the uncomfortable feeling you're treating this like some sort of counterspy adventure.'

He recoiled as though I'd slapped his face, which was approximately the reaction I'd been hoping for. 'I didn't mean to,' he said. 'I'm sorry, Mr. Tobin, I didn't—'

'I know you didn't,' I said, willing to take him off the hook now that he'd learned the lesson. 'You just have to be more careful not to act quite so elaborately innocent and conspiratorial. Unless you're already known as an outgoing and extroverted personality, sitting at this table was itself a mistake. Trying to talk to me about what I'm doing here was a second mistake in such a public place, and being so obviously furtive about it was a third. We're just having a conversation, you and I, the sort of chat two people might have who have just met. There's nothing to look secretive about.'

'You're right,' he said, but of course he couldn't avoid looking crestfallen, another out-of-place expression. Happily, no one seemed to be paying much attention to us. 'I am sorry,' he said.

'And if I'm going to call you Bob,' I said, trying to relax him, 'you'll have to call me Mitch. All right?'

A happy smile spread over his features. At last, a non-suspect expression. 'Sure it's all right,' he said. 'Mitch.' And insisted on shaking hands, which I resigned myself to putting up with, extending my left hand across my body for him to grasp awkwardly and pump with his right.

Stoddard brought us our swordfish a minute later, and it too was very good. The fork was even more confusing left-handed than the spoon had been, but I managed.

While we ate, I asked Gale to fill me in on the quartet I didn't know, the four women at the table across the way. I had to warn him against sneaking sly glances in that direction, but after that he settled down and gave me their names.

And it turned out I was at last in the presence of two of the injurer's victims. The woman facing me was Rose Ackerson, and the one on the left was Molly Schweitzler, they being the two women who'd been bruised and burned when a table in this room had collapsed on them during a meal, the first of the faked accidents.

Though I already knew the histories of both women, and they were hardly among the suspects anyway, I allowed Bob Gale to tell me the blend of fact and fancy he knew about their backgrounds. Rose Ackerson, a woman in her late fifties, had been three years a widow when suddenly she'd kidnapped an infant from a baby carriage outside a drugstore. She had cared for it well, had made no attempt to get any ransom, and when caught she had tried to claim it as her own child. She'd spent the last four years in a state mental institution.

Molly Schweitzler, a plump woman of forty-three who looked like a somewhat overly solemn earth mother, had never been married. She currently weighed less than at any time since the age of fourteen. Her family had had her under psychiatric care since she was nineteen, and so far she'd been inside mental hospitals eleven times, for a total of not quite fifteen years out of the last twenty-three. She had attained weights in excess of four hundred pounds, had often literally eaten herself sick, and her mother had reported more than once seeing Molly still trying to eat while in the middle of vomiting. She weighed about two-hundred-sixty now, had been institutionalized for the last sixteen months, and the prognosis of the doctors was poor. No one seriously expected her abused body to survive more than another ten years – the heart would probably give out first – and it was more than likely at least part of that time would be spent once again inside an institution.

The other two women at the table had not as yet fallen foul of the injurer. One was Ethel Hall, thirty-seven years old and extremely tall and thin, who had also never been married. She'd been a professional librarian since graduation from college, and was thirty-five when she sexually attacked an eleven-year-old girl, who reported the incident to her parents. It turned out not to be the first child thus approached by Miss Hall, though it was the first time any child had told anyone about it. The girl's father went to Miss Hall, full of angry threats, and after he left she slit her wrists. It was only because the father decided to go to the police that she was found before she could die.

Why is it that tragic life stories so often seem to have a thread of comedy, almost of farce, running through them? I don't know. I only know that faces, eyes, even hands are a more than sufficient antidote to the impulses of antic humor. Watching the small careful birdlike movements of Ethel Hall as she picked at her lunch, it was hard to find anything funny in the idea of the lesbian librarian.

The last woman at the table was Marilyn Nazarro, a young woman now twenty-seven. She had married while still in high school, though apparently not out of the traditional necessity, since it was nearly two full years before her first child was born. A year later she had twins, and shortly after their birth a vague depression began to settle over her. It deepened quickly, and soon the three children were being cared for in the homes of their grandparents, since Marilyn had become incapable of caring for them. She was sleeping and eating poorly, rarely getting up and never getting dressed, she was weeping frequently, and ultimately she took to soiling the bed. At that point the family doctor decided it was time to call in a psychiatrist, and two weeks later Marilyn was committed to a sanitarium, where she stayed two years, then a year of freedom, then another three years in the sanitarium, ending two months ago. The doctors did not believe they had found and eliminated the cause of the depression, and they expected to see Marilyn Nazarro again.

Looking at her, a chipper vivacious brunette, looking younger than twenty-seven, brightly made-up, the sparkling conversationalist of that table, it was hard to believe she wasn't cured forever; but I knew that the majority of mental patients who have been hospitalized once will be hospitalized several more times, and the odds are good that the final commitment will be permanent. Marilyn Nazarro with her recurrent depressions, Molly Schweitzler with her recurrent bouts of eating, both were very much of the usual type of mental patient, who could be compared to a kind of wind-up doll. The sanitarium winds them up and sets them loose in society, where they gradually run down again, and have to be returned to be wound up once more, over and over while the spring gets weaker, until the time comes when they can't be wound up any more at all, and they never again step outside the walls.

That made me think of my own wall, and that I wouldn't be able to work on it until my arm was healed. That gave me a sudden queasy feeling, as though I were on a bobbing boat which had just lost its anchor.

FIVE

Doctor Cameron read the note aloud: ' "Sorry it was you".' He turned the paper over and looked at the blank side, then looked at me. 'With a bottle of Scotch?'

'A small bottle, yes,' I said. 'The seal hadn't been broken, so I doubt it's been tampered with.' Bob Gale and I, fresh from lunch, were sitting in front of the desk in Doctor Cameron's office. I would have liked to spend longer in the dining room, till I'd seen everyone, but there was too much else to be done, including reporting this note. I had handed it over upon arrival, as the first order of business.

'Very strange,' he said. He put the note on his desk, face up, and frowned down at it. 'Very very strange.'

'I take it none of the other victims has received this kind of note,' I said.

'None at all, this is the first time. I don't understand it.' He looked at me. 'You're assuming it's from whoever is doing these things.'

'I think it most likely,' I said. 'Not necessarily so, but likely. The note doesn't claim to be from the one who rigged the staircase. In fact, it doesn't even claim the staircase was rigged. You could read it to be simply an expression of good will from someone who was sorry to see me get hurt. Sorry to see anybody get hurt.'

Doctor Cameron shook his head. 'An anonymous expression of sympathy. No, it doesn't seem likely.'

'It's *bound* to be from the guilty one,' Bob Gale said. He was sitting on the sofa along the right-hand wall. 'There's nobody else it *could* be.'

I turned and looked at him. 'It's not a hundred per cent. It's ninety per cent, it's enough so we can take a chance on making the assumption. Particularly if there haven't been any other expressions of sympathy like this after the other accidents.'

'None,' said Doctor Cameron.

I said, 'I don't mean necessarily a note. Maybe a gift, like the Scotch, left anonymously in the victim's room.'

'Someone would have mentioned it,' the doctor said. 'No, there's been nothing like this before.'

'All right,' I said. 'Then that leads us to the question, why this time? If it is from the injurer, why didn't he want me in particular to be caught by his booby trap?'

'Maybe because you just got here,' Bob Gale said. 'You weren't really one of us yet, or something like that.'

'I suppose that's possible,' I said. 'But it's more likely he or she knows who I am and why I'm here.'

'I don't see how,' Doctor Cameron said.

I said, 'Either you or Bob must have mentioned it to somebody else. Somebody you could trust, not necessarily the injurer, but some innocent third party who then went and passed the story on in confidence to somebody else, who told somebody else, and by now maybe half the residents know about it.'

Gale said, 'Mr. Tobin, I swear to you I haven't said a word to anybody, not a word. I know I acted silly in the dining room just now, but that was because I was excited that you were here, and I promise you that's the only time I've slipped. And I didn't tell anybody. I wouldn't. I promised Doctor Cameron I wouldn't, and he'll tell you if I give him a promise I stick to it.' He was so serious and open it was impossible not to believe him.

Doctor Cameron said, 'No, Mr. Tobin, that isn't the answer. I'm sure Bob didn't say anything to anyone, and I know for certain I didn't. I haven't even told Doctor Fredericks, and I certainly don't suspect my own assistant. But I knew that what you just said was likely to happen. I would tell one person, who would tell one person, and so on. Doctor Fredericks might have one specific individual here he felt needed to be warned against the danger, and he would tell that person, and the chain would be well on its way. That's why I didn't even let it get started. And I impressed just that very point on Bob. No, your secret is still a secret.'

Doctor Cameron's reasons for keeping his assistant in the dark sounded strained to me, and had from the beginning, but there was no point trying to decide what his real reasons were until I'd met the assistant, Doctor Lorimer Fredericks. So I said nothing about that, but stuck to the issue at hand. 'Why me?' I asked. 'Why apologize for snaring me, and not apologize for snaring anybody else? Look at the note again, it makes the point crystal clear. It doesn't merely say the sender is sorry, he's sorry it was *me*. If it isn't because he knows the truth about me, why is it?'

Doctor Cameron spread his hands. 'Mr. Tobin, why is he causing these accidents in the first place? His motivations are obviously irrational, so how can I guess for you what his reasons are for regretting having hurt you? Perhaps Bob is right, this person feels you're too much of a newcomer, and you aren't part of the family or tribal group, however he thinks of it, and he's sorry that an outsider got hurt in the course of family trouble.'

'I don't know,' I said. 'It may be something like that, I can't be sure. That doesn't sound exactly right, though.'

Doctor Cameron said, 'I don't mean to tell you your business, Mr. Tobin, but I doubt this is a case where you'll be able to deduce motive first, and then find the perpetrator. I think this time we'll have to find the perpetrator first, and once we have him we'll be able to ask his motive.'

Bob Gale said, 'What about fingerprints, Mr. Tobin? Do you think there might be some on the note?'

'I doubt it,' I said. 'Paper doesn't take prints well, and in any case they'd most likely be mine. Amateurs have known enough to wear gloves for at least twenty years now. And even if we did find a legible print on there that was neither mine nor Doctor Cameron's, I doubt it would be a good idea to line up all the residents and take their fingerprints.'

'For some of them,' Doctor Cameron said, 'it would be a very bad experience indeed.'

'And at the end of it,' I said, 'it might turn out the print belonged to a clerk in a stationery store downtown.'

Bob blinked and grinned. 'I'm sorry I asked,' he said.

I said to him, 'There's a question I've been meaning to ask you. Were you by any lucky chance in the ping-pong room when Debby Lattimore came and got Jerry Kanter to show me to my room?'

'Sure,' he said. He grinned again, saying, 'I would have shown you up myself, only I was in the middle of a game and it would have looked funny to quit.'

'I'm glad you realized that,' I said.

'Oh, I'm not always as dumb as I was at lunch.'

'I'm sure you're not. Who was your opponent yesterday?'

'Well, there were three of us playing. You know, the man out this game would play the winner next game. It was me and Edgar Jennings and Phil Roche.' Naming two of the residents I hadn't as yet seen.

I said, 'Were the three of you still playing up to the time I had my accident?'

'Oh, sure. We were set for the afternoon.'

'Good,' I said. 'Did either of the other two leave the room at all from the time Jerry Kanter left till I had my accident?'

He frowned, thinking back. 'I'm pretty sure they didn't.'

'That's fine,' I said, and turned to Doctor Cameron to say, 'We've just started the process of elimination. Neither Jennings nor Roche set the trap I stumbled into.'

He didn't understand. He said, 'How can you be sure?'

I told him about the small nail hole I'd found in the baseboard last night, and of my feeling my ankle had caught on something just as I started to fall down the stairs. 'Whoever set it,' I said, 'had to be nearby to remove the evidence right after the trap was sprung. Also, it wasn't there when Jerry Kanter and I came up those stairs, so it had to be set at some time while Bob here was playing ping-pong with Jennings and Roche. Bob was already eliminated, so now we can eliminate Jennings and Roche.'

'And two more,' Bob said. 'Marilyn Nazarro and Beth Tracy were in there watching the game, and neither of them left.'

Marilyn Nazarro was the young lady who'd looked so vivacious at lunch but whose history was of crippling depression. Beth Tracy I hadn't yet seen.

'That's even better,' I said. 'That's five eliminated, plus the people who've been injured, which would be Mrs. Ackerson and Molly Schweitzler with the table that collapsed, Donald Walburn with the ladder, Miss Wooster with the terrace, and George Bartholomew with the bed frame in the closet. For a total of ten, out of twenty-one.'

'Twenty-two,' Doctor Cameron said. 'If you're counting Miss Wooster. She's in the hospital now, and there are twenty-one people here without her.'

'Very well,' I said. 'Ten from twenty-two. Leaving twelve residents, plus Mrs. Garson the cook and Doctor Fredericks your assistant.'

'You aren't counting those two as suspects, I hope.'

Until I saw them – particularly until I saw Doctor Fredericks – I wasn't counting them out, but I didn't say that. I said, 'Probably not. By the way, which of the residents has the nickname Dewey?'

They both looked blank, and Doctor Cameron said, 'None that I know of. Why?'

'I met him last night. He told me his nickname was Dewey.'

Doctor Cameron shrugged a little and said, 'Every once in a while, a resident will regress a little. Particularly at night. I

37

would guess offhand it's someone who was nicknamed Dewey at some other period in his life, and that former time was prominent in his mind last night. But I wouldn't know which one it was.'

I said, 'I'd like to be able to put the faces and the dossiers together, so if I'm ever with either of you and I say, "Dewey", please look where I'm looking and tell me what name he goes by in this period of his life.'

They both assured me they would, and then Doctor Cameron said, 'Now that you have your list of suspects down to twelve, what are you going to do next?'

'Wander around,' I said. 'Meet more people. You have group therapy sessions every day, don't you?'

'Twice a day,' he said, 'morning and afternoon. It's voluntary, and very lightly attended, but some of the residents are reassured by the idea that it's there if they ever need it. I take the morning sessions, usually, and Doctor Fredericks takes the afternoons.'

Bob Gale said to me, 'You're going this afternoon, aren't you?'

'Of course,' I said. I lifted my right arm, in its cast. 'After my experience yesterday,' I said, 'it's only natural I'd want some reassurance.'

Three P.M., group therapy, in a large square room with bookcase-lined walls. A large oval table dominated the room, flanked by armless wooden chairs with padded leather seats and backs. By two minutes before the hour there were seven of us seated at the table, well-spaced, no two people sitting directly side by side. Doctor Fredericks had not yet arrived, and both ends of the oval table were unoccupied, so I didn't yet know which end was considered the head.

The six others included some faces I already knew, plus some new ones. The ones I knew were Molly Schweitzler, the fat lady eliminated as a suspect because she'd been one of the first two victims, plus Jerry Kanter, who'd shown me to my room, and either Robert O'Hara or William Merrivale, one of the two young men I'd first seen washing the station wagon. The new faces were two women and a man, all more or less middle-aged.

There was very little conversation. Jerry Kanter was in low-voiced but animated discussion with O'Hara/Merrivale – I was looking forward to learning which of those two was which – but the rest of us simply sat in silence, glancing at our watches and waiting. It reminded me for some reason of a Roman Catholic church I'd once been in on a Saturday afternoon. The people sitting in the pews next to the confessionals, waiting their turn to tell their sins to the priest, had worn much this same look of vaguely worried introspection.

Which in turn reminded me of Linda Campbell, because it had been with her that I'd gone into the church. I'd sat in the rear pew, alone, and waited while she went to confession, and I'd wondered what she would have to say to the priest about me. 'Father, I am a married woman having an affair with a married man.' Or, worse: 'Father, I am having an adulterous affair with the policeman who arrested my husband and is responsible for him now being in jail.'

Not that Dink Campbell had been railroaded by me in the role of some sideshow Solomon, not at all. Daniel 'Dink' Campbell was a professional burglar, and he was guilty of the crime I arrested him for and a judge sent him over for. But I, after Dink's arrest and imprisonment, became guilty of sleeping with his wife.

I tried not to think of Linda Campbell these days – or Jock Sheehan either – but somehow the atmosphere in this room was conductive to poking at aching teeth, opening old sores, relighting the purgatories of the past. I was deep in the chain of events that had led to my dismissal from the force and my present life of limbo when the door opened once again and Doctor Lorimer Fredericks walked in.

He could have been no one else. He was a youngish man, about thirty, and he carried himself with a prim confidence and self-assurance that no recent mental patient could possibly bring off. He wore a tweed jacket with leather elbow patches, dark trousers, brown walking shoes and a green shirt open at the throat. His head was small and fine-boned, with black hair slicked straight back. He sported a thin pencil moustache and a look of such complete self-satisfaction that I detested him on the spot, and began at once to try to find some motive for Doctor Cameron's assistant to be guilty of causing the accidents. Trying somehow to squeeze the doctor out and take his place? Running some sort of psychiatric experiment of his own? The ideas that popped into my head were nonsensical and I knew it, but that was the effect the man had on me.

He took a seat at one end of the table, thereby making that the head, and we all watched him carefully take a pair of horn-rimmed glasses from his jacket pocket, clean them with a handkerchief held between thumb and first finger, and then use two hands to precisely fit the glasses to his face. He then flashed a brisk professional meaningless smile around at us all and said, 'Not a bad turnout today.' He looked at me. 'You're the new man, aren't you? Tobin.'

'That's right,' I said.

'I understand you've had an accident.'

I was sitting there wearing a pajama top, with my cast-enclosed arm sticking out the bottom at my side, which made the fact of the accident fairly obvious, but I understood he had merely used a polite form of statement. Still, just about anything the man said could immediately get my back up. I quelled an impulse to be sarcastic, saying only, 'Yes. I fell and broke my arm.'

'Is this the first time you've ever broken a bone?'

It was. I'd been shot in the leg once, seven or eight years ago when I was still on the force, and had spent five weeks in the hospital, but no bone had been broken. 'Yes, it is,' I said.

He studied me with impersonal interest through his horn-rims. 'Do you recall what you were thinking as you were falling down the stairs?'

Here was an unexpected problem. Doctor Fredericks not being privy to the truth about me, he was unconsciously skirting close to areas of questioning I might have trouble finding the right answers for. Hoping he'd switch to someone else soon – after all, this was supposed to be *group* therapy – I said, 'I guess I was just frightened.'

'That's all?' The eyes seemed to glint behind the glasses. 'No feelings of guilt? You weren't blaming yourself for having been clumsy?'

'I wasn't clumsy,' I said, but this line of questioning was difficult to deal with. I tried to think what my reactions would have been if it had been a true accident. Would I have been angry at myself for stumbling? Probably, it would only be natural. But not very angry, and not guilty. But what was I to say, beyond the denial that I'd been clumsy. Lamely I said, 'It was just an accident.'

He smiled, a large false smile that made me think of an animal trainer who's just gotten a fairly stupid dog to roll over on command. 'Very good, Tobin,' he said. 'You understand why I asked that, of course.'

I didn't, and I suppose I just looked blank.

'Because of your history,' he reminded me, frowning slightly. 'Wasn't it an overpowering feeling of guilt that sent you to Revo Hill in the first place?'

Then I remembered the false background Doctor Cameron and I had prepared. It had made me someone who believed he was responsible for the death of a co-worker – as in fact I was – and who had become unable to function as a result of the conviction of his own guilt. (The false background had been uncomfortably close to the truth in a number of ways, but Doctor Cameron had assured me it would be much easier for me to behave like a facsimile of myself than as, for instance, a suicidal transvestite or an irresponsible schizophrenic.)

So I said, 'I've gotten all over that. That's why they let me out of Revo Hill.'

'I'm glad to see they were right,' he said. 'Since you're the new man, would you like to fill the others in on your background, how you happen to have been at Revo Hill and so on?'

Which was just exactly the sort of detailed question I

couldn't possibly handle at all. Doctor Fredericks would see through me first, and some of the others might also smell a rat. Mental patients would know whether someone in their midst was a real mental patient himself or not, unless he kept his mouth discreetly shut. I said, 'I'd rather not today, Doctor. I just got here, and had the accident, and I'm feeling a little shaky still.'

He frowned at me again, more thoughtfully this time. I knew it was a false note I'd just struck, that the whole concept of group therapy is built on the fact that mentally sick people enjoy describing their symptoms just as much as physically sick people do, and that it wasn't properly in character for me to attend this session and not want to talk, but this was the lesser discrepancy when compared to the Swiss cheese I'd create if I tried to narrate my fake history to these people. So I had to remain silent.

Doctor Fredericks said, 'Then why did you join us today?' Exactly the question I knew I'd raised in his head.

I said, 'I wanted people around me, I guess. I didn't particularly want to be alone.'

Up till now, the other six residents had merely sat and watched the doctor and me, their eyes on whichever one of us was talking, but not one of them joined the conversation. It was Molly Schweitzler, the fat woman, who was sitting across the table from me. Almost glaring at me, as though in some sort of challenge, she said, 'Did anybody laugh at you?'

I looked at her, not understanding the question but relieved at distraction in any form. 'Laugh at me?'

'When you fell,' she said.

'Nobody was there when I fell,' I told her. 'The people I've seen since then have all been very kind. Nobody's laughed at all.'

Doctor Fredericks, thank God, hared off on this new scent, saying to Molly Schweitzler, 'Why should anyone laugh at a man with a broken arm?'

'Well, they sure laughed at Rose and me,' she said, 'when that table broke on us.' She turned back to me. 'That was about a month ago,' she said, 'and I still got bruises on my legs.'

Doctor Fredericks said, 'Molly, no one laughed when they found out how serious the situation was.'

'No, they had their fun first, and then they came around to see if Rose and me were okay.'

Doctor Fredericks was off in hot pursuit of this new quarry by now, and it was with a great feeling of relief that I sat back and let the hunt go on without me.

Molly Schweitzler's feelings of having been laughed at when she'd hurt herself were easily plumbed, of course. A grossly fat woman like Molly could hardly go through life without running into cruel humor now and again, and of course in overeating Molly was hurting herself, just as much as when the table had hit her. Her anger at the laughter that apparently really had gone around the dining room when the table first gave way was really much older anger than that. She was angry at all the people who had been funny at her expense all her life, and angry at herself for never having done anything about it. She'd never fought back, never stood up for her own dignity, and she had the angry frustration of someone determined to fight back when the last round is already over.

Still, however obvious Molly's misplaced anger, it proved interesting to the group at large, and led to a discussion which shortly switched to another woman, Doris Brady, whom I was seeing for the first time. Doris Brady was a young woman suffering from a fairly recent addition to the list of mental illnesses, called culture shock. She had joined the Peace Corps at twenty-seven, after a childless marriage of five years had ended in divorce, and was sent to one of the most backward and poor of the emerging African nations. She was expected to be a schoolteacher, in a society so totally different from anything she'd ever known before that her mind was incapable of encompassing it. This doesn't happen frequently, and the Peace Corps people try to weed out ahead of time those to whom it might happen, but when it does occur it is a brutal and terrifying experience. Doris Brady had found herself suddenly cast adrift, between two cultures neither of which she could any longer see as viable. The values and assumptions she'd grown up with in the United States had been swept away by the realities of the African village to which she'd been sent, but the values and assumptions of the village were too alien for her mind to live with. Life without some safe bedrock of accepted truths is insupportable for most people, among them Doris Brady. From what she was saying now, as the focus shifted to her from Molly Schweitzler, the hospital where she'd spent the last three years had done an adequate job of rebuilding her faith in the assumptions we live by in the United States.

43

The session lasted two hours, and in that time everyone present got a chance at the limelight. I found it fascinating to sit and listen to them, watching them reveal themselves a thousand times more freely than if they'd known they were suspects being observed by a hired ex-cop.

I finally got to resolve the O'Hara/Merrivale problem, when the one in this room turned out to be William Merrivale, the young man who had once tried – almost successfully – to beat his father to death. He had never been as sick as his home situation, and the last year in a private sanitarium had helped him primarily by giving him somewhere other than his own home in which to live. Now The Midway was performing the same function, and it developed in the conversation that he was still ambivalent about where to go and what to do when his six months' stay here was ended.

So if this was Merrivale, the missing one must be Robert O'Hara, who had begun his career as a child molester while still a child himself, and could never for very long keep his hands off little girls. O'Hara and Merrivale were both twenty-one, the two young males at The Midway, both blond and muscular, both looking like Marines or college football players.

The day twelve years ago when Jerry Kanter took a rifle downtown and killed seven people he'd never met before was so distant in his mind these days that he didn't even mention it. All he wanted to talk about was his brother-in-law's car-wash operation, and was the brother-in-law trying to cheat Jerry, and would Jerry be happier working for strangers who didn't know about his past, and so on and so on. He was still chipper and cheerful, the same spry little man who'd first showed me to my room, but even though I knew he'd been insane and not in control of his senses on that day twelve years ago, I kept thinking of those seven dead people and wondering about their questions about brothers-in-law and job opportunities and the rest of it, clicked off now, silent forever. And the man who'd clicked them off was now cured, happy, cheerful, weighing his possible futures. The seven, unfortunately, were incurable. I knew it was an unfair reaction, but I disliked Jerry Kanter intensely all the time he was talking.

The last two new faces turned out to belong to Nicholas Fike and Helen Dorsey. Nicholas Fike was forty-three and looked seventy, a man who had gone from simple alcoholism to mental collapse. The only trouble was, he'd done it twice now, and neither his body nor his mind was up to that kind of punishment. He talked with a very bad stutter, blinked constantly, and was in an obvious agony of self-consciousness whenever Doctor Fredericks asked him a question. Why he'd come here when it was such plain torture for him I couldn't guess, unless it was some belief that if he forced down every bit of bad-tasting medicine he could lay his hands on, sooner or later a cure would result.

Helen Dorsey was forty-five, a stocky, brutally girdled matron with a harsh voice and a tendency toward playing the drill sergeant. She was clearly trying to control that tendency, with only limited success. Four years ago, when the last of her three sons had departed for college, Helen Dorsey and her husband sold their house and moved to a smaller ranch-style house in a new development section outside their city. Helen had always been a neat housekeeper, but in the new house she gradually became obsessive about it. Her husband would wake in the middle of the night to find her scrubbing the kitchen floor. Late the next summer, with the two still-unmarried boys home from college and overcrowding the little house, Helen Dorsey went berserk, driving husband and sons from the house, barricading herself in alone. The police had to go in after her, and now, three years later, she was deemed sufficiently in control of herself to be released from the sanitarium.

The pecking order in the session was also interesting. Helen Dorsey, bossy and perfectionist, pecked everyone except Molly Schweitzler, the fat woman, who in her turn pecked only to counterattack and was therefore mostly left alone. Jerry Kanter pecked everyone but Molly and Helen, but was himself occasionally pecked by William Merrivale. Doris Brady and Nicholas Fike, the culture shock victim and the alcohol victim, were pecked by everyone and pecked no one, not even each other.

Doctor Lorimer Fredericks was somehow simultaneously separate from the pecking order and deeply a part of it. He pecked away at everybody from the security of his position as psychiatrist, and yet he went overboard so consistently that he was frequently pecked right back, particularly by Molly Schweitzler and Helen Dorsey. William Merrivale betrayed a sullen desire to turn Fredericks into a substitute father two or three times, his clenching-unclenching fists on the table demonstrating that the paternal hostility was still very much alive. Jerry Kanter tended to express his irritation the most openly, and thus to get rid of it more quickly than the others, turning irritation into a joke more often than not. Doris Brady

45

and Nicholas Fike both merely wilted before Fredericks' tongue until rescued by someone else, usually Helen Dorsey.

I couldn't understand how someone with a personality as generally repellent as Doctor Fredericks' could possibly hope to get anywhere in psychiatry. In a way, I was pleased to see that my reaction to him was echoed by everybody else, but on the other hand it seemed to me the man's manner could only wind up doing more harm than good. It seemed to be bringing out Helen Dorsey's worst characteristics, for instance, and at the same time confirming Doris Brady's belief in her own inadequacy.

By the time the two hours were up, I was about convinced that whoever was setting these booby traps was doing so purely in hopes of sooner or later catching Doctor Fredericks. I determined to go directly from the session to Doctor Cameron and find out if he had any idea how his assistant treated the residents.

But when the time was up and we all started to leave, Doctor Fredericks said, 'Mr. Tobin, would you mind staying on a minute? It won't take long.'

What wouldn't take long? I stood where I was, and the others filed out, and the two of us were alone.

Doctor Fredericks took off his glasses and leaned back in his chair. He put one wing of the glasses in his mouth, a gesture I have always thought pretentious and stupid. He said, 'Sit down again, why don't you?'

'If this won't take long—'

'It'll be even shorter,' he said, 'if our heads are at the same level. Do sit down.'

So I sat down. Why was the man so irritating? What I really wanted to do was hit him in the mouth.

He studied me cavalierly for a minute, and then said, 'I don't know what it is about you, Tobin. I've read the reports on you, of course, and you just don't stack up. You're hiding something, or faking something. Or you're afraid of something. Is that it? Are you afraid somebody here will decide you really shouldn't have been released yet, and we'll bundle you up in a restraining jacket and ship you back to Revo Hill? Is that the matter?'

'It's just that everything's strange here, that's all,' I said. The damn man was offensive, but he was sharp. His narrow nose had smelled something.

46

He shook his head. He said, 'You don't behave like an overawed newcomer. You behave more like a spectator in a zoo. You feel superior to the rest of the residents, don't you?'

I had to deny that, naturally, and I did, but of course I automatically had felt superior. After all, I'd never had a mental breakdown, I'd never had to be hospitalized, though God knows there'd been strain enough. But my problems hadn't defeated me, not entirely. I'd adapted. I'd found a way to survive. So yes, I did feel superior to the other residents, but without tipping my hand I couldn't tell Fredericks so, or tell him why.

In fact, it had long since become ridiculous to go on keeping Fredericks in the dark, and if he hadn't been such an offensive personality I would have told him the truth long before this. But that finally explained why Doctor Cameron hadn't told him, a question that had been puzzling me. Now I could see why he'd chosen to follow his own counsel and not expose his ideas to the insulting contemplation of his assistant. I was sure it had been that, and nothing to do with security, that had kept him from confiding in Fredericks.

But why keep Fredericks around at all? Still, I supposed a psychiatric assistant for a place like The Midway might not be an easy post to fill. Doctor Cameron himself was here out of a labor of love, The Midway being his own creation, but an assistant would have to be here only as one step in his career. And wouldn't the best men go to hospitals and sanitariums, where the real work needed to be done, rather than to a halfway house for the more timid former patients? Only the dregs would be left for Doctor Cameron to choose from, and Fredericks was the result.

At any rate, he brushed aside my denial of superiority feelings, saying, 'I watched you throughout the session, Tobin, and you saw yourself as merely an observer, not a participant at all. You watched the others as though they were putting on a performance for your amusement.'

'Not at all,' I said, and couldn't add, 'not amusement but enlightenment.'

'Don't lie to me, Tobin,' he said.

I said, 'Don't talk to me like that, I'm not one of your—'

He cocked his head to one side. 'What was that?'

'I'm new here,' I said, feeling embarrassed and foolish and frightened. 'I'll take part after I'm used to the place.'

'You're not one of my what, Tobin?'

I shrugged, and looked away. 'I just don't like the way you talk,' I said.

'Am I too alert for you?'

He was, damn him. I shrugged again, not looking at him.

'You prefer negligence, is that it?'

If I were actually what my dossier said, that would have been a low blow, since the fake story was that my negligence had caused the death of a fellow worker. I looked at him, furiously trying to think of what the proper response would be from the Tobin he thought I was, but all I could say was, 'Fredericks, you're a true bastard.'

He leaned forward, staring hard at me, his left hand tapping his glasses on the table top. Another irritating habit. He said, 'You're being an observer again, Tobin. What's with you?'

'Nothing's with me.'

In a beautiful shot in the dark, he snapped, 'Did you cause a co-worker's death?'

'Yes,' I said.

'How?'

For some reason, I have no idea why, I blurted out the truth. 'I was in bed with a woman.'

He frowned, staring at me. There was nothing like that in anything he'd read about me. 'In bed with a woman? What difference did that make?'

'I should have been with him, to back him up. He was my partner, and I should have been with him, but I was with this woman. I spent a lot of time with her, I'm married, I had to do it while I was on duty, sneak off to see her and Jock would cover for me. My partner.'

Watching me carefully, he said, 'What happened?'

'He went to pick somebody up. Jock did. It should have been a simple easy pick-up, but it went wrong, and Jock got killed, and they found out I wasn't with him.'

'Who found out?'

'The force.' But I heard at last what I was saying, and looked away from Fredericks' eyes. 'I'm getting a headache,' I said, though I wasn't. 'I'm not sure what I'm saying.' Though I was.

'Tobin.'

I looked at him, very reluctantly.

'Tobin,' he said, leaning very close to me, staring into my eyes, 'Tobin, who the hell are you?'

I met his eyes, trying to find an answer, and there wasn't any. I listened to the silence, and knew there wasn't anybody around to fill it but me. I shook my head at last and said, 'I think we better go talk to Doctor Cameron.'

Doctor Cameron did the talking, and Doctor Fredericks sat there and listened. When we'd first walked in, I'd told Doctor Cameron just enough to let him know the time had come to break security with Fredericks, and then I'd sat back and let him take over. Fredericks was like a sponge with a knife-edge, if there can be such a thing. He absorbed it all, every nuance and implication.

When Cameron was done, Fredericks said, in a controlled but shrill voice, 'Why wasn't I told before this?'

'I thought it best to have the knowledge as narrowly confined as possible,' Cameron told him. It was interesting to see how much Cameron himself disliked Fredericks. 'I thought it would be easier for you to go on as usual if you thought things were as usual.'

'But don't you see what this does?' Fredericks was enraged, but was keeping a tight lid on his fury. 'It absolutely destroys the purity of what I'm trying to do. You should have been in that session today, Doctor, you could just *feel* that something was out of kilter. I knew it had to be Tobin, I knew there was a false note of some kind in him, but I never for a minute suspected he'd been inserted *deliberately*. It nullifies everything I'm trying to do if an uninvolved spectator takes part in group therapy. Even having him in the building—'

Doctor Cameron began to soothe Fredericks' ruffled feathers, assuring him that one wax apple wouldn't spoil the bunch, while I sat back and watched in pure amazement. Of all the reasons Fredericks could have found for being angry now – and I could think of several – he had chosen one completely out of left field. He wasn't upset to think he hadn't been told what was going on. He wasn't upset that the danger to the residents was still alive without their being warned of its existence. He was only upset because my presence altered the conditions of some obscure ongoing experiment he thought of himself as carrying out. The Midway was for him nothing but a laboratory, and if the inmates wanted to spend their time hurting one another that was merely interesting; if the man in charge wanted to keep secrets from his assistant that was merely irrelevant; but if someone not in accordance with the standard resident profile was surreptitiously inserted into the mix, it put him into an absolute pet.

I sat and listened for quite a while, as Fredericks fumed and Cameron cajoled, until Fredericks flung out his arms and cried, 'How can I judge their reactions to *me* when they are subconsciously reacting to *him*?' Pointing at me.

I said, 'Doctor Fredericks, excuse me.'

He looked at me, angry and impatient and intense.

I said, 'Do you have the idea in your head that you're offensive to the residents on *purpose?*'

He made an angry brushing-away gesture, saying, 'I have neither the time nor the inclination to explain my techniques to laymen.'

'That isn't a technique, Doctor Fredericks,' I said. 'You've been just as offensive to me since finding out I'm not a resident as you were before. You know damn well Doctor Cameron isn't a resident, but you're steadily offensive to him.'

Doctor Cameron patted air in a peacemaker's gesture, saying, 'That's all right, Tobin. Doctor Fredericks and I understand one another. We'll work this out.'

'I'm glad,' I said, and struggled to my feet, not easy onehanded. 'I'll be up in my room, resting. I'm still a little shaky from yesterday. Let me know if I should pack or not.'

Doctor Cameron's expression appealed to me for forbearance. 'I'm sure everything will work itself out,' he said.

I nodded, seeing in his face that I was only making it all more difficult for him. I wouldn't have said anything at all except that Fredericks had managed so unerringly to rub me the wrong way, and I now restrained myself from saying any more.

Too bad Fredericks couldn't. As I started for the door he said, 'Tobin.'

I stopped and looked back at him.

He said, 'You don't think my manner is a technique. How many people have you told on first meeting what you told me?'

'I didn't say you weren't effective,' I said. 'I simply said it wasn't a technique. A technique is something you can put on and take off. A shark's teeth are effective, but they're hardly a technique. They're simply something he has because he's a shark.'

Fredericks offered me a flinty smile. 'Under other circumstances,' he said, 'a long train ride, say, I would probably enjoy talking with you, Tobin. But not here. I don't expect *you* to understand that, you aren't a professional, but Doctor Cameron should certainly—'

'Watch that,' I snapped. 'Doctor Cameron is standing right there, if you want to talk to him face him and talk to him direct.' I looked at Doctor Cameron, standing behind his desk and looking pained. 'I'll be in my room,' I said, and left the office.

Debby Lattimore was bent over her paperwork in the outer office, as usual. Had she heard anything of the argument? I stood near the closed door for a few seconds, but could hear no conversation through it, so Debby was probably still unaware of the problem of my real identity. Which was good, since she was technically still on the active list of suspects, though I found it incredible to think it might be her.

She looked up and gave me a distracted smile as I went by; I returned it and went out to the hall.

Traveling through The Midway was a constantly unnerving experience, only partly because of the maze-like confusions of the place. The main point, though, was the danger of booby traps. Who knew what unsprung traps were lying around waiting for a victim? I tried to move normally, not to seem odd to the people I passed, but I tended to shuffle and stick close to the walls, like a blind man.

It took a while once again to find my way to my room, and the problems and dangers of the search worked wonders in getting me off my irritation. When I finally walked safely into the room I no longer had any particularly urgent desire to hit Doctor Fredericks in the mouth. I still thought of him as offensive, a naturally offensive man who had found a way within his occupation to turn a personality defect to advantage.

The strange thing was that I didn't resent his having gotten me to talk about myself. In that regard, I trusted him. I had no doubt he would never use against me what I'd told him. Unless I was in the position of patient, of course, when he would surely hit me over the head with it from time to time just to see what my reactions were. He struck me, all in all, as being one of those medicines worse than the disease it cures.

I was physically weary, but mentally alert, which meant I was soon bored inside my room. Aside from having promised to be here when the doctors had finally straightened things out between them, I really didn't feel up to wandering around at all, seeking out someone to talk to or anything like that. Within the room there was virtually nothing to occupy my mind, no radio or television set, nothing to read.

Finally, for something to do more than out of any belief I would learn anything, I decided to make a list of the residents, dividing them into those still suspect and those already cleared. I sat at the writing desk with my notebook and pen, and when I was done I had three lists. After the names of those I'd already met I put down some fact about the person to help remind me which one was which. I could have done so with the others, but I was afraid of reducing them too much to an adjective before actually seeing them.

The first list was of the five people other than me who'd so far been injured:

Edith Wooster	(terrace)
Rose Ackerson	kidnapper widow (table)
Molly Schweitzler	overeater (table)
Donald Walburn	(ladder)
George Bartholomew	(closet)

The second list was also five names long, and was those residents accounted for during the time the stair booby trap had been laid:

Bob Gale	shell shock
Edgar Jennings	
Phil Roche	
Marilyn Nazarro	depression
Beth Tracy	

And the third list, those residents still suspect, ran to twelve names:

Jerry Kanter	multi-murderer
Debby Lattimore	suicide/catatonic
Robert O'Hara	child-molester
William Merrivale	father-beater
Kay Prendergast	nymphomaniac
Walter Stoddard	killer of retarded daughter
Ethel Hall	lesbian librarian
Doris Brady	culture shock
Nicholas Fike	alcoholic
Helen Dorsey	compulsive housekeeper
Ruth Ehrengart	
Ivy Pollett	

Of these twenty-two people, I had so far met fourteen, but most of the eight I was yet to see in person were already eliminated for one reason or another. Edith Wooster, for instance, was still in the hospital following the collapsed terrace. Donald Walburn and George Bartholomew, neither of whom I'd yet run across, had both been involved in accidents. I hadn't seen Edgar Jennings or Phil Roche or Beth Tracy, but they were among those eliminated by placement when the stairs were rigged. That only left Ruth Ehrengart and Ivy Pollett among the active suspects still to be seen in the flesh.

I did already know both women, of course, to some extent, from the dossiers Doctor Cameron had loaned me. I no longer had them, since they would be difficult to explain in my room if someone else stumbled across them, but in my eighteen years on the force I had trained myself to have a good memory for material like that, and I remembered the general outlines of the histories of both Ruth Ehrengart and Ivy Pollett.

Ruth Ehrengart was thirty-seven now. Between the ages of nineteen and thirty-one she'd had ten children, all still living. She had begun to be treated medically for extreme nervousness at twenty-seven – merciless comedy wants to edge in here, but I'm sure one look at Ruth Ehrengart's face will cure that – but the nervousness increased, aggravated by frequent, almost incessant colds. In her thirtieth year a manic-depressive cycle started, its swings at first too long and gentle to be noticed, but then growing more severe, the happy periods verging on hysteria, with insomnia and boundless energy, the downs getting ever lower, with the nervousness giving way to violent irritability or a deadening depression. Shortly after her thirty-second birthday, she took the family car after Mass one Sunday, drove to a highway, and traveled at excess speeds till a state trooper spotted her. She didn't stop for his siren, but simply went faster than before, the chase at times exceeding one hundred miles an hour and ending at a roadblock set up ahead of her. Her manner with the police and court officials led to her being held over for psychiatric examination, which ultimately led to her voluntary commitment to an institution. Five years later, the institution considered her stable enough to be returned to society, a judgment she obviously wasn't sure she agreed with or she wouldn't be here at The Midway.

Ivy Pollett's problems were almost the exact opposite. A spinster now forty-two, Ivy Pollett had lived with her chronically ill mother all her life, until four years ago she went to the police to declare that a grocery delivery boy had raped her. The boy, when picked up, denied the charge but wasn't believed until several days later when Miss Pollett went back to the police station to report that her mailman was a Communist spy. When questioned further, it turned out that virtually all the people Miss Pollett came in contact with were spies or rapists or escaped convicts or white slavers. She was aware of a plot being hatched among these people to do away with her because she'd found them out, and when she realized the detectives questioning her were also part of the plot she became hysterical. It had taken four years in a state institution, during which time the chronically ill mother had died, before Ivy Pollett became convinced that she was not at the hub of an intricate plot.

Thinking of these two women and looking at my lists, it occurred to me I'd already met all my male suspects, which meant Dewey from last night had to be on one of the cleared lists. Which was good; he'd seemed harmless enough, and it was pleasant to have him not a suspect.

Well, which one was he? There were only four men on those two lists I hadn't yet seen, so it was one of those four he had to be. Donald Walburn, George Bartholomew, Edgar Jennings, Phil Roche. I considered the names and dossiers, trying to guess which one would turn out to be Dewey.

Well, it wouldn't be Donald Walburn, who'd broken his leg with the rigged ladder, because Walburn was still going around on crutches. And George Bartholomew, who had been hit in the face by the metal bed frame, still bore the marks of that accident, so it couldn't have been him either.

Edgar Jennings. One of the ping-pong players with Bob Gale. Also, before his commitment, a self-exposure on New York City subways. His routine had been to wear a raincoat and a pair of cut-off trouser legs that only reached up to the knee, where they were held by rubber bands. When the raincoat was closed, he seemed to be fully dressed. His habit was to open the raincoat and expose himself to the people in a subway car just before the doors were shut, then jump out onto the platform while the witnesses were all whisked away to the next station.

But Edgar Jennings was thirty-two years old. Dewey was older than that.

Which left Phil Roche. But Phil Roche was a man who'd suffered most of his life from an inferiority complex, in part created and very much aggravated by a defect he had as a result of an illness in infancy. A shriveled left arm, with a useless tiny hand dangling from it higher than his waist.

Dewey hadn't had a shriveled left arm.

There had to be something wrong somewhere. I frowned at my lists, I made check marks after all the male names, I counted the lists of names, and it always came out the same. I hadn't left anyone out, I had every one of the twenty-two names written down there, of the twenty-two there were only four men I hadn't yet met, and it was absolutely physically impossible for Dewey to be any one of them.

So who the hell was Dewey?

EIGHT

They were still at it, Cameron and Fredericks, when I walked in without knocking, and they both looked at me in irritation. But I didn't care. If it had been going on for half an hour since I'd left, and they could both still have those expressions on their faces, there was no point in my being polite and waiting till they were done before I spoke to them.

Cameron said, very testily for him, 'Tobin, we're still in the middle of—'

'You two can work that out later,' I said. 'But I think I'm onto something important.'

Fredericks said coldly, 'Tobin, when you left here you offered to wait in your room until we decided what would be best—'

'I'm really tired of you, Fredericks,' I said. 'You aren't going to shut me up, but unless you're very careful I *will* shut you up. So just sit down and be quiet for a minute.' In Fredericks' stunned silence, I turned to Cameron and said, 'Do you remember I mentioned to you a resident named Dewey that I met last night? This morning, really.'

Fredericks was looking at me in bewilderment, still trying to think of something applicable to say, so Cameron had an opportunity to answer the question, which he did ungraciously. 'I remember the conversation,' he said. 'And I remember telling you I had no idea which of the residents he was. I still have no idea. If you want to know who he is—'

'He isn't anybody,' I said. I understood that Cameron was in a foul mood because of Fredericks, and I didn't take offense.

Cameron closed his mouth and frowned at me. Fredericks acted as though he was just about deciding to become superior and bored and walk out on the scene. I said, 'You have ten male residents here now, and Dewey isn't any one of them. Do you understand what I'm saying?'

'No,' Cameron said, and Fredericks, smiling slightly, said, 'Tobin, you wouldn't be in the process of inventing an extra little mystery here, would you, to keep your employment alive?'

I continued to look at Cameron. 'He's a fool,' I said, 'but you're not. You know how little I wanted this job in the first place. Besides, I already mentioned Dewey earlier today, before any question about my job came up. Whether I pack or not, the fact remains that at five o'clock this morning I met a man in the second-floor hall of this building who was neither of you two and who was none of the male residents, but who knew the building intimately, who led me to the kitchen and actually made my breakfast for me, who told me he likes to meet the new arrivals and chat with them, who told me most of the history of The Midway, and who said I should call him Dewey. If he wasn't either of you and he wasn't any of the male residents, then who in the name of God was he?'

Cameron had been standing, leaning forward slightly with his fists pressed down on his desk top, but now he settled slowly backward into his chair while Fredericks stared at the two of us, trying to decide whether I was to be believed or not.

Cameron said, wonderingly, 'I don't know who he was. I don't know who he could possibly have been.'

Fredericks said, 'Are you trying to tell us somebody came into this building last night and wandered around the halls, pretending to be a resident?'

'Not at all,' I said. 'He didn't come in last night, he lives here.'

Fredericks turned to Cameron with a gesture of exasperation. 'He isn't making any sense,' he complained.

Cameron said to me, 'You just said he wasn't any of the residents. Now you say he lives here.'

'Both are true,' I said. 'You have the landlocked equivalent of a stowaway somewhere in this building. I don't know who he is, I don't know whether or not he's responsible for the accidents, but I do know he's unofficially living here.'

'That's impossible,' Fredericks said, and Cameron said, 'That's fantastic, Tobin. Are you sure it isn't just someone who wandered in off the street?'

'He was dressed in cardigan, work pants and scuffed old sneakers, very much an at-home kind of clothing. But more important than that, he knows this building. He knows it physically, he's the one who led me to the kitchen, and did it directly, no mistakes or detours. He's prepared a lot of meals in that kitchen, because he made our breakfast in obvious comfort with his surroundings. He didn't open any wrong cabinets to find plates or coffee or whatever. And he chatted about the place, its history and the people here, he knows The Midway as well as either of you two. And he told me he likes to meet new people shortly after their arrival and chat with them about the place.'

'Then why didn't anybody ever notice him before?' Fredericks asked.

'I'm sure other people have noticed him. But you have a constant changeover of residents here. If I were a normal resident, I wouldn't think anything was strange about my having met Dewey, and I wouldn't have any reason to think it was strange if I never happened to run into him again. I've been actively moving around trying to meet people, and there are still eight residents I haven't met. Under normal circumstances, by the time I would meet everyone here a couple of people would be leaving and one or two new ones would have arrived. My one encounter with Dewey would quickly fade from my mind, and if I did ever think of him again I'd just take it for granted he'd finished out his six months and left.'

Frowning heavily, Fredericks said, 'I just can't swallow it. Where would he hide? How could he possibly live here and not be seen?'

'This is a large building,' I said. 'When I first came here, Debby Lattimore told me there'd been some thought of making a map of the place for new residents, but no one knew the building well enough to draw it. I'm sure there are a dozen odd corners where a stowaway could set up housekeeping.'

Cameron said, 'But it doesn't make sense. Why would anybody want to do something like that? A stowaway is someone who wants to take a trip but doesn't have the money to pay his fare. This building isn't traveling anywhere.'

'It's traveling through time,' I said. 'It could just be somebody who wants to live here.'

'But why? Why does he want to live here under such constricting circumstances?'

'I don't know,' I said. 'When we find him, we'll ask him.'

Fredericks said, grudgingly, 'I suppose we have to believe you, Tobin. It's too pointless a story to be made up.'

'It's too easily checked, too,' I pointed out. 'If Dewey exists, if I saw him, there's no reason we can't find him again. As a matter of fact, there's another way we can check. Debby was in the outer office when I came in. Would you call her in?'

'Certainly,' Cameron said. 'Why?'

'Ask her if she remembers Dewey. If she remembers meeting him shortly after she first came here. A man in his early fifties, small-boned, wire-framed glasses, very mild manner, full of stories about The Midway.'

Cameron nodded, and picked up his phone. He dialed one

number, and asked Debby to come in. As he was hanging the phone up she walked in, and he said, 'Debby, do you remember ever meeting a man named Dewey here?'

She frowned. She glanced at me in some curiosity — my activities had to be confusing — but devoted most of her attention to the question. 'Dewey? A resident?'

'Yes. A mild-mannered man of about fifty. He liked to talk about the history of The Midway.'

'Oh!' she said, abruptly smiling. 'Him! Sure, I remember him. He wore those funny glasses with thin metal frames. They're very in now, you know.'

Cameron and Fredericks looked at one another, and back at Debby. Cameron said, 'When did you first meet him, Debby?'

'Just the one time, I think. Once or twice. I guess that would be just before he left.'

'When was that?'

'A couple of days after I first got here,' she said. 'In March, I think. I got a vacuum cleaner from downstairs, to do my room, and he popped up out of nowhere and helped me carry it upstairs. Then he sat around in my room for an hour or more, talking while I cleaned the room up. Gee, that would be the day after I got here, I cleaned the whole room. He told me just about everything I know about The Midway.'

Cameron said, 'And you haven't seen him since?'

She frowned, thinking back. 'I don't think so. Maybe in the hall sometime, I don't know. I guess he must have left just after that, he sounded as though he'd been here a long time already.'

Fredericks said, a trifle too sharply, 'Didn't that strike you as odd?'

She looked at him, puzzled. 'Didn't what strike me as odd?'

'That you only saw him the one time.'

'No,' she said, and shrugged. 'Why should it?'

Cameron, with more sense than Fredericks, said, 'There's no reason, Debby, thank you very much.'

She looked around at us all, more and more puzzled. 'That's it?'

Cameron solved what could have been a sticky problem by saying, 'Yes, that's all, thank you. If you'd gotten to know him better, you might have been able to give us your impression of him, but since you just saw him the one time there's really no point in it.'

The explanation didn't fully make sense to her, mostly be-

60

cause Fredericks' question had been a jangling error, implying problems that Cameron's explanation didn't cover. And also, of course, because of my unexplained presence, the new man sitting at his ease in Doctor Cameron's office while the two doctors are asking unusual questions. But the disparity wasn't strong enough to make her pursue the question further, so she left, puzzling, and I knew she would sit out there in the other office thinking about it for quite a while, which was unfortunate but unavoidable.

When we three were alone again, Cameron said, 'All right, Mr. Tobin, you've made your point.' I was pleased to see the *mister* come back in front of my name; it had disappeared during Cameron's argument with Fredericks.

Fredericks still wanted to fight. He said to Cameron, 'Which means we have two outsiders living here, not just one. How can we do anything of therapeutic value in an uncontrolled situation?'

I said, 'All situations are uncontrolled to one extent or another, except death.'

He glowered at me, angrier with me than ever now I'd been proved right. He was like those ancient kings who responded to bad news by killing the messenger who'd brought it. He said, 'I'm still not looking for understanding of technical problems from a layman, Tobin. I'd appreciate it, when Doctor Cameron and I are talking, if you wouldn't put your two cents in.'

'Sorry,' I said, and got to my feet.

Cameron said, 'Where are you going?'

'Back up to my room to wait some more.'

'But what about this man Dewey? What are we going to do about him?'

'Doctor Cameron,' I said, 'you're talking like a layman. There are still technical problems to be worked out first. Once you and Doctor Fredericks decide what you think about the environment and the controls and all that, let me know if you still—'

Fredericks snapped, 'Come off it, Tobin, don't act like a spoiled brat. There *are* other problems besides yours, you know, and—'

'And you aren't one of mine, Doctor Fredericks,' I said. 'And you aren't going to be. I refuse to go into competition with you for Doctor Cameron's affection. I've been hired for one specific job, and that's—'

'That's the most asinine—'

'All I'm going to do, and if—'

'Competition? Do you actually suppose that you—'

'I'm not wanted for that job I'll be happy to—'

'Gentlemen!' Doctor Cameron was on his feet, waving his arms at us, shouting over our shouts. 'Gentlemen, please!'

'You've got a goddamn inflated idea of yourself, Tobin, is all I can—'

'I'll be happy, I say,' I repeated, louder, 'to pack up and get the hell out of this semi-bedlam and wash my hands of the whole thing.'

'Gentlemen! Please, gentlemen!'

'You,' Fredericks shouted at me, 'with your typical police mentality, all you can think of is tracking down some troubled mind as though you were hunting alligators in a swamp. Why wasn't I *told* what was going on?' He rounded on Cameron suddenly, shouting, 'Why wasn't I asked for assistance? Doctor Cameron, I *know* these people, I know their *minds*. Don't you think I could find the one who's doing these things?'

Cameron was very unhappy. 'I thought,' he said, moving his hands vaguely, 'I thought professional help was the answer.'

'Professional help? *Professional* help? I don't particularly want to insult this man Tobin, but in what way would you say his roaming around here since yesterday could be called professional help? The man's first act upon entering the building was to break his arm!'

'Now, that's unfair, Lorimer,' Doctor Cameron said, 'and you know it. Besides, look what he's done already, he's discovered Dewey, this man Dewey, living in our midst and none of us even knew about it.'

'Discovered him?' Fredericks looked elaborately around the room. 'I don't see him.'

'Discovered the *existence* of Dewey.' Doctor Cameron had more patience than I would have. 'Lorimer, I can understand your being upset, but there's no justification for being unfair. We both know that Mr. Tobin was angry when he spoke to you the way he did, that the charge was nonsense, and I'm sure he already regrets having made it.'

I did, as a matter of fact, though I wouldn't have agreed that the charge was nonsense. But I was willing to go along with the part of the sentence I did agree with, since it had occurred to me it was foolish to stand around exchanging small arms fire forever with Doctor Lorimer Fredericks, so I said, 'I do regret it, it was said in the heat of battle. I'm sorry.'

Fredericks too had apparently decided enough sniping was enough. I'd spoken to Cameron, but Fredericks treated it as though I'd apologized directly to him, saying, 'That's all right, Tobin. I understand the impulse to lash out, I've fallen victim to it myself once or twice.'

That was supposed to be a joke, but even Fredericks' jokes made me want to go for the jugular. I restrained myself, though, and even managed a small and entirely false smile.

'Now,' said Cameron, obviously rushing in before anybody could start up again, 'the most important thing to discuss is this man Dewey. And the two questions are, it seems to me, how do we find him and is he the one responsible for the accidents?'

'He's the most likely,' Fredericks said. 'Whatever his reasons for hiding in here in the first place, they're probably involved with his reasons for setting the traps.'

I didn't think it was as sure a thing as that – Dewey just hadn't struck me as the right kind of person for the job – but there was no point starting the ruckus all over again so I didn't disagree with Fredericks directly, I merely said, 'We'll know better once we've found him.'

Cameron said to me, 'How do you propose we do that?'

'We'll have to recruit Bob Gale,' I said, 'and the four of us start in the basement and work our way upstairs. Spread out enough to keep Dewey from slipping past us into the part we've already searched, and yet close enough together to remain in contact. It'll be tricky, but we can do it.'

Fredericks said, 'And what will the other patients think of our skulking through the corridors? Or do we let them know what's been going on?'

'I don't think we should,' I said. 'Just in case Dewey's innocent. And we ought to run our search late at night. That's when he takes to moving around himself, I think, so he'll be likelier to run across then. And the other residents won't be awake to notice what we're doing.'

Doctor Cameron said, 'What time do you think we should start?'

I said, 'Well, I ran into him—' and the door burst open.

We all turned and looked, and it was Debby Lattimore, with Jerry Kanter looking agitated in the background behind her. 'Doctor Cameron,' she said. 'There's been an accident.'

NINE

My list of suspects was now reduced by one. Kay Prendergast, twenty-two years old, three illegitimate children while still in her teens, compulsive and apparently joyless sexual promiscuity, all of which seemed to have been bleached out of her in five years inside a sanitarium, was now lying on the floor of her room, crumpled into a coma on her side, with wine dark blood oozing slowly out onto the floorboards from under her head.

It was plain to see what had happened. A small black-and-white television set was twitching away to itself on a table, in that nervous jumpy manner television has when it's running but no one in the room is watching. It was Kay's own set, The Midway having no money for radio or TV sets in the residents' rooms. Across the room, near the window, was a brown wooden captain's chair, with a back that curved around to form the arms. Kay had come upstairs, turned on the TV, walked across the room, and sat down in her chair. The left rear leg had then collapsed, dropping her backwards, and her head had hit the radiator under the window.

Doctor Cameron was brisk and efficient: 'Debby, call the hospital. We need an ambulance. Tell them it's an emergency.'

'Yes, Doctor.'

The room was crowded already, and Debby had to push her way through to the door. I stood to the side, near the television set, out of the line of sight between the spectators and the victim, and watched their faces. Among them were several of my suspects, like Walter Stoddard, the mournful Norman Rockwell character, my waiter at lunch. And Helen Dorsey, the battle-ax, the compulsive housecleaner. And Doris Brady, the culture shock victim. And Robert O'Hara, the husky blond all-American type who was a repeated child-molester. And Jerry Kanter, the multi-murderer who concerned himself these days with his brother-in-law's car-wash operation.

I looked at their faces, and I tried to find an inappropriate expression in one of them. Satisfaction, perhaps, or amusement, or even anger. But there was nothing at all. Walter Stoddard simply seemed more mournful than ever, with a kind of despairing pity for the injured girl. Helen Dorsey also had pity in her face, a frowning pity that wanted to be active, to clean up, to briskly put things right somehow. Doris Brady looked mostly frightened and repelled, as though the sight of an injured body was a new challenge to the eternal verities she'd so painfully recaptured. Robert O'Hara looked pained, as though his comprehension of what had happened to Kay was overpowered by the dreadful knowledge that the same thing could happen to him. And Jerry Kanter looked helpful and sympathetic, the kind of good neighbor who always helps out in emergencies but whose passions are somehow never engaged.

There were also some of the other victims present. Rose Ackerson and Molly Schweitzler, the two women whose table had collapsed, stood together, looking down at the body and then around at the other spectators. as though comparing the reaction to this accident with the laughter at the time of their own. But theirs had been the first accident, and this one was obviously much more serious, and no one this time was laughing.

There was also someone new to me, and from the angry fresh scars around his mouth and across his right cheek he would be George Bartholomew, who had been hit with the bed frame when he'd opened the storage closet door. A short man in his early forties, George Bartholomew was a saver, a string collector, newspaper hoarder, garbage keeper. He was also a kleptomaniac, constantly stealing from stores small items for which he had no desire or use, and it was his kleptomania which had attracted him to the attention of the authorities. When his house had been searched for the things he'd stolen, it was found to be crammed, room after room, with old newspapers, stray pieces of furniture, bags of rotting garbage, piles of old clothing, odds and ends of every imaginable type. The junkman who eventually cleaned the place out for the new owners subsequently reported having removed, among other things, over four hundred dollars' worth of deposit bottles.

Why George Bartholomew had been released after nine years in an institution I had no idea, unless it was a case of overcrowding and of releasing the least violent and dangerous patients. George Bartholomew was hardly cured, though he did limit his kelptomania to stores and never stole from people he knew. But it had been in fact his magpie or pack rat personality that had led him to open that rarely used closet in the first place. I looked at him now, and on his battered face was

65

nothing more than a meek man's helpless sympathy for some-one who'd been hurt.

There was a brisk discussion taking place between Helen Dorsey and Doctor Cameron. She wanted Kay picked up and put on the bed, to make her more comfortable, but Doctor Cameron didn't want her moved until the ambulance team arrived and could determine the extent of the girl's injuries. While the talk went on, I continued to watch the faces, and then noticed that Doctor Fredericks was watching mine.

I met his eye, expecting him to look away, but he continued to study me, the skepticism in his expression deepening into a kind of angry and humorous challenge. He was clearly saying, *Here is another of your failures, what are you going to do about it?*

Could it be him after all, could it possibly be him? I was like a poor poker player then, holding a hand that intelligence said should be folded, and yet studying it, studying it, trying to find some combination of cards and possibilities that would justify staying in the hand just a little longer. I wanted Doctor Fredericks to be guilty, he had the personality for it and it would soothe me tremendously if he were actually the one, but I knew it was stupid and fruitless to dwell on him, that my injurer was elsewhere.

In this room? What was the likelihood of the injurer coming to look at what he had done? Whatever satisfaction he found in causing pain and injury to his fellow residents, wouldn't it be increased by actually looking upon the result of his labors? I looked again at the faces around me. Walter Stoddard, Helen Dorsey, Doris Brady, Robert O'Hara, Jerry Kanter, all from my active list. Some sort of unreasonable motive could be worked up for any one of them, which wasn't much help, and there was nothing in any of their faces to offer me a hint or a suggestion. The only faces showing anything other than variants on sym-pathy, in fact, were those of Rose Ackerson and Molly Schweitzler, who weren't even among my suspects, and whose preoccupation with the reaction to this accident was under-standable, given the general reaction to their own.

Helen Dorsey, thwarted in her desire to move Kay Prender-gast onto the bed, made up for it by moving the rest of us out of the room instead. 'We've all seen enough,' she said briskly. 'Let's go on about our business now.' And herded us all out to the hall.

Groups almost always obey orders given in a loud confident

voice, and this time was no exception. We all trailed outside. Most of the others were reluctant, but I was just as glad to be away from the unconscious girl and the skeptical eyes of Doctor Fredericks. While the rest stood around in chatting pairs and trios in the hall, I walked away from them and headed for my own room, moving with the reluctant watchfulness of a man threading his way through a minefield, which in many ways is exactly what I was.

I didn't try to do any coherent thinking until I was in the safety of my own room, and then I found myself wondering about Dewey again. I'd been automatically rejecting him from my list of suspects, but that really wasn't a sensible thing to do. He was at least a stowaway, and who knew what else he might be? And why was I so resisting the thought of him as a possible suspect?

I lay on my bed, frowning at the ceiling, and concentrated on Dewey, forcing myself to think past my conviction of him as a gentle and harmless little man, forcing myself to find out why I thought about him the way I did. And I finally decided there were two reasons for it. First, Doctor Fredericks had at once jumped to the assumption that Dewey was our man, and I would tend inevitably to take the other side in any dispute involving him. It was true that Fredericks had come off that initial assumption somewhat, claiming an open mind until we could find Dewey and question him, but the first impression was still there, and very strong. And secondly, Dewey was somehow a teammate of mine, a fellow tribe member or some such thing. Not only were the two of us the interlopers here, the ones who didn't belong and who were keeping the truth from general awareness, but I had also felt in him some kinship with my own mental set, as though there were some connecting link between my desire to build my wall and his desire to stow away inside this building.

But neither reason was good enough. Someone was setting these traps, and if it was true that some sort of unreasonable motive could be worked up for any of the people on my suspect list, it was just as true that the same thing could be done with Dewey. Even more readily, in fact, since I knew so much less about him. I mean by that, I could give him any motive I wanted for living hidden away in this house, and it wouldn't be hard to connect it with a motive for hurting the bona fide residents.

Starting, of course, with the fact that they *are* bona fide residents, as he is not. Or with the idea that he wanted the building to himself and was jealous of anyone else living here.

The point was, there were too many questions about Dewey to leave him off the suspect list. I'd done so out of emotional reasons, which was stupid and unprofessional, and it should at least be possible for me to remain professional.

It was the place, somehow, the aura and atmosphere of The Midway itself. The feeling of sitting on a powder keg. of never knowing when the next accident would be rigged, or what form it would take, or who it would hit. Plus the people themselves, all of them still trailing hints and echoes of their past disturbances. And Doctor Fredericks, who for reasons best known to himself had turned rejection and disapproval into a high art.

I got up from the bed and went over to the writing table and got out my lists, that I'd made earlier today. I was startled by them at first. having forgotten how different and how odd my writing was left-handed. It looked like the work of a child, or a disturbed adult.

I had changes to make on the lists. Holding the paper steady with the cast on my right arm, I crossed Kay Prendergast's name off on the suspect list and wrote it in on the bottom of the injured list. Then I paused, feeling great reluctance still, but finally went back to the suspect list and wrote at the bottom:

DEWEY

Someone was sitting on my arm. I was lying stretched out on a park bench, very late at night, and someone was sitting on my arm. It didn't really hurt, but I couldn't move the arm and it was annoying. And then a policeman came along and began to shake my shoulder, wanting me to get up and move along. He thought I was a bum, and I felt very embarrassed and ashamed, thinking how once I had been on the force and now this young rookie was looking down on me for sleeping on a park bench.

I opened my eyes, and Bob Gale whispered, 'It's four o'clock.'

'I was on the force once myself,' I said apologetically, 'but there's someone sitting on my arm.'

'Mr. Tobin,' he whispered, and shook my shoulder again, staring into my eyes. 'Wake up, it's four o'clock.'

'Oh,' I said. 'Yes. I'm sorry, I was dreaming.' I pushed myself up to a sitting position. 'I'll be right along,' I said.

'All right,' he whispered. 'Be seeing you.' And he tiptoed out of the room, closing the door carefully behind himself.

I felt so old. I pushed the covers off with my good hand and put my legs over the side and got heavily to my feet, and every movement was accompanied by the creaking and aching of my joints. Bob had turned on an overhead light and I stood squinting beneath it, wanting not to be called upon.

But there was no choice. It turns out there never is a choice, only the occasional illusion to keep us interested. Life is ten per cent carrot and ninety per cent stick.

I dressed, in my clumsy awkward way, and went down the hall to the bathroom to wash my face one-handed, an unsatisfactory experience. The frustration woke me more than the water did, and by the time I shuffled back to the room to fill my pockets and switch loafers for slippers I was awake again and capable of a limited interest in what was going on around me.

Kay Prendergast had been taken away to the hospital with a skull fracture. I had napped for a while in the afternoon, and had Jerry Kanter and William Merrivale and Bob Gale for dinner companions. The room was full, almost all the residents tending to take dinner at the same time, but it seemed to me unusually quiet for so many people. This final accident, the sixth in less than a month, had apparently been the critical one, pushing a kind of awareness suddenly into everybody's mind at once. I had noticed many of the residents glancing at my injured arm, thoughtfully. None of them had any definite suspicions yet, but a feeling of trouble was in the air. They were like a herd of deer suddenly smelling something in a stray breeze.

Jerry Kanter, in fact, had been one of the few people in the room oblivious to the general aura, and I found myself wondering if this blithe insensitivity of his was a form of padding given him in the process of his cure or if it was a natural element of his personality, perhaps the element that had made it possible for him to take that rifle downtown that day. The murder of people you know requires emotion, but the murder of perfect strangers requires a dull insensibility.

At any rate, Jerry had chattered happily throughout dinner, while the rest of us at the table, feeling the general tension, sat mostly silent. William Merrivale, the father-beater, had sat sullen and rebellious most of the time, head down, throwing occasional mulish glances at Jerry as though he'd like to shut him up by direct means. Bob Gale had been kept silent not only by the atmosphere in the dining room but also by his all-too-apparent fear of inadvertently exposing our conspiracy, a fear that communicated itself to me and made me even more nervous than I was already. All in all, I was just as pleased when dinner was finished and I could get out of there.

I had spent the evening in various public rooms, watching ping-pong or reading magazines or whatever, getting into brief conversations with other residents whenever I could do so without seeming to push too hard. I was trying for nothing more than to get to know my suspects a little better, and had ended the evening with no further enlightenment.

About ten o'clock the two doctors and Bob Gale and I had met in Doctor Cameron's office. Doctor Cameron told me Kay Prendergast's chair showed the marks of having been tampered with, and Bob Gale said it had to have been done recently as there was still sawdust on the carpet under where the chair had stood. Doctor Fredericks moved that we call in the local police at once, as no one present seemed capable of doing anything constructive about what was an extremely dangerous situation, but he wasn't serious about it, merely turning the knife, and when we ignored him he didn't pursue the question.

We had discussed Dewey, and the fact that he had to be considered a prime suspect, and that the first order of the day was to get hold of him and question him, either to remove him if he turned out to be the menace in our midst, or remove him from the top of the suspect list if he should turn out to be innocent. I had suggested that the best time to go in search of him would be very early in the morning, before anyone else was up, when I had seen him the last time, and Bob Gale volunteered to get himself up and the rest of us awake by four o'clock. We would then meet in Doctor Cameron's office and start our search from there, traveling in pairs.

So now it was four o'clock, and after five hours of uncomfortable and restless sleep I didn't at all want to go downstairs to Doctor Cameron's trusting patience or Doctor Fredericks' needling or Bob Gale's boyish eagerness. Once again I was thinking of home, and more particularly of my wall, and I regretted the fact that there hadn't been a train back to New York right away when I'd arrived in Kendrick. I would have no broken arm now, and no complicated relationships with other people, and no troubled mind to concern myself with but my own. The house would be empty for a month, I could have it all to myself, and wouldn't that right away lighten the burden? However sincere was Kate's forgiveness, however much she truly cared for me and truly wanted to help me, there was no way she could avoid being a reminder of what I'd done and what had happened to me as a result.

Maybe I'd been too hasty in my estimation of Walter Stoddard's wife. But then again, all estimations of human beings are too hasty, no final judgment can ever be made, there's always more to learn, more colors to alter the portrait.

What would the portrait of Dewey be, once I found him again? Wondering that, I left the room and went down the hall and at the first turn there was Dewey, standing there with a small patient smile on his face, obviously waiting for me. 'Hello, Mr. Tobin,' he said.

'Hello,' I said, trying to show nothing. We had intended to search in pairs exactly to avoid this sort of situation. I was not, one-armed, going to be able to capture Dewey. Nor did I want to frighten him into hiding. 'Off to get another midnight snack,' I said.

'May I walk with you?'

'Delighted,' I said.

71

He fell in beside me and we walked toward the rear stairs. He was subtly different from what I remembered, like a second signature from the same person, almost identical but not quite. He seemed somehow less harmless, more mysterious and unknown, his smile less honest, his body less weak. Of course, on that first meeting I didn't know he was a stowaway, and this time I did. Knowing there was in fact something very strange. Whether this was the full explanation, or if in fact he was more menacing tonight, I had no way to tell for sure.

We walked to the stairs in silence and started down them, and he said, 'Did you find your ring?'

I drew a blank. 'I beg your pardon?'

'The ring you lost when you hurt your arm,' he reminded me. 'You were looking for it when we met.'

Then I remembered the quick lie I'd invented last night, and I said, 'Oh! No, no I didn't find it. I don't know what happened to it.'

We reached the foot of the stairs and he opened the door, saying, 'Well, of course, it didn't exist. That's why it's so hard to find.'

I stepped through and looked back at him. He came through and shut the door and smiled amiably at me and I said, 'What do you mean?'

'I knew you were fibbing all along, Mr. Tobin,' he said. 'When someone wears a ring all the time, there's always some sort of mark on their finger, but you don't have any marks at all. And if you did have a ring and you lost it, you would have looked at the bottom of the staircase instead of at the top. I know you're on your way to Doctor Cameron's office, but why not walk with me to the kitchen first? I'd like to talk with you, if you don't mind.'

I was flabbergasted, and could think of nothing to do but go along with him. 'Sure,' I said. 'I'll walk with you.'

'Thank you,' he said.

We started off, toward the kitchen, and I said, 'You're quite a detective, Dewey.'

'I think that's what you are,' he said, and gave me his mild smile again. 'I think you're a detective in disguise.'

'Not a very good disguise,' I said.

'Oh, yes, it is,' he assured me. 'I'm sure no one else guesses at all. I just had a special reason to be wary, that's all.'

'So does the person I'm looking for.'

'That's what I want to talk with you about,' he said, and

held the kitchen door open for me. We went into the kitchen together and he said, 'Would you like a cup of coffee?'

'No, thank you.'

'I'm making a pot anyway.'

'All right, then, thank you.'

I sat down at the table, and he began to get out the things he needed. It was exactly like last night, except that now we knew much more about one another. But the echo was strong, as though somehow lost innocence was represented by this repetition of a pleasant interlude under ambivalent circumstances, and I felt oppressed by the duplication.

As he made the coffee he talked. He said, 'At first, I couldn't think I was right about you, because why would a detective be here at The Midway in disguise? Then I thought it was perhaps some District Attorney somewhere was afraid that psychiatry meant narcotics and free love, but you just weren't the right sort of man to be looking for illicit pleasures in a place like this.' He smiled at me, sharing with me the idea of his joke, and went on: 'Then I thought it perhaps was me you were after, but of course that was mere paranoia. In the first place, I was certain absolutely no one knew I was here. And in the second place, you didn't behave last night as though you were looking for someone who isn't legally here and who prowls mostly at night. You weren't suspicious of me, and if you were looking for such a person you would have been.' He turned to me again, his smile self-deprecatory. 'I'm not a true detective,' he said, 'despite my lucky observation about your ring. I can only go by the way people feel to me.'

'That's the best way to be a detective,' I said.

'Is it?' He sounded both pleased and interested. 'I thought that might be your way,' he said. 'I'm sorry to say I searched your room. I didn't steal anything and it wasn't to be malicious, it was just because I was curious about you. And you had no detective things at all. Nothing for fingerprints, no handcuffs, no cameras, nothing at all.'

'I'm not that kind of detective,' I said.

'I can see that.' He had the coffee on, and now he came over to sit across the table from me. 'It'll be ready in just a minute. Now. I didn't believe you were looking for immorality, and I didn't believe you were looking for me, and you didn't have any detective apparatus, and for a while I thought I must be wrong. What were you looking for?'

I considered telling him, to see his reaction, but decided to wait and let him guide the conversation himself. He was obviously headed toward some particular point, and I was very interested in finding out what it was.

He said, 'I couldn't think of a thing until yesterday afternoon, when poor Miss Prendergast fell and hit the radiator. I was thinking what a coincidence that was, first you having an accident and breaking your arm and then Miss Prendergast falling and hitting her head against the radiator, and then I remembered there'd been *other* accidents, and I suddenly realized they weren't accidents at all! Someone was doing them on *purpose!*'

He seemed honestly shocked, even offended, his usually mild eyes staring at me through his wire-framed glasses as though insisting that I too should be affected by this piece of news. I said, 'That's true, Dewey. Somebody is doing them on purpose.'

'But that's *awful!* I don't know if you, an outsider, can realize just how awful that really is.'

'I think I realize,' I said.

He either didn't hear me or didn't believe me. 'This place is a haven,' he said. 'It is safety, security, protection. Not like the outside world. For someone to be cruel in *here* – no, it can't happen, we can't let it happen!'

He was getting agitated, eyes staring, pale hand closed into a fist and shaking above the table. I said, 'I think the coffee's perking.'

He looked around at once. 'Yes.' He got to his feet and went over to the stove. 'A minute or two more,' he said, and went to get our cups.

As he set the table I told him, 'I agree with you, Dewey, this place should be safe from that kind of wanton cruelty. And you're right, that's what I'm here for, to find out who's doing it and make him stop.'

He was bringing milk over from the refrigerator. He put it on the table and said, 'I knew you would suspect me. That's only natural, I'm here in an unusual way. I knew you'd want to know everything about everybody, and it wouldn't take you long to discover the man you'd met last night wasn't any of the regular residents. So that's why I wanted to talk with you now, before you could do anything about it.'

He went over to the stove and got the coffee and brought it to the table. He poured two cups, put the pot on a trivet, and sat down again. 'I want you to know it isn't me,' he said. He was speaking very softly and earnestly, watching his hands as he added milk and sugar to his coffee. 'I want you to find the person right away,' he said, 'so I don't want you to spend all your time thinking about me.' He looked up, met my eyes. 'It isn't me,' he said.

I believed him, but I didn't say so. I said, 'But you're a stowaway.'

'Stowaway?' He smiled, surprised and pleased by the word. 'Stowaway,' he said again. 'That's nice.'

'Naturally,' I said, 'that makes you very much of a suspect.'

'Oh, I know that.' He was earnest again, looking directly at me. 'I can't go anywhere else,' he said. 'Please don't expose me, they'll make me go away and I don't have anywhere else to go. And I'm not the one, I swear I'm not. I'll help you look for him, if you want me to. I know this house, I can keep an eye out now that I know what's going on. But please, please don't expose me. It won't do any good, I'm not the one doing all these things. Please.'

I couldn't meet his eyes, they were too full of pleading and helplessness. Using the excuse of sipping at my coffee, I looked away from him and said, 'You can't go on like this anyway, you know. Doctor Cameron knows you're here, I've already told him.'

'If you don't look for me,' he said, 'they'll forget. If you find the person doing the bad things, and then you go away, everyone will forget. I'll keep right out of sight, and they won't even think about me.'

'It wouldn't work,' I said. 'Besides, what do you want to live this way for? Wouldn't it be better to be in the open?'

The thought terrified him, and he made no effort to hide the fact. He didn't say anything, he merely stared at me and shook his head.

I said, 'I'm sorry, Dewey, there's nothing I can do about it.'

'You'll hunt me down?'

'Why do we have to? Come along with me now to Doctor Cameron's office. You know Doctor Cameron, don't you?'

'Of course.'

'You know he's a fair man, you know he'll do whatever he can for you.'

'The only thing to do for me,' he said passionately, 'is leave me alone. I'm not hurting anyone, I'm not in anyone's way. I just want to be left alone. Can't you believe I'm not the one you want?'

'I do believe it,' I said. 'But I believe it because I've talked to you. Talk to Doctor Cameron and he'll believe you, too. But if he doesn't have the chance to talk to you, he's got to be suspicious.'

'You could convince him.'

'I'm sorry.'

He studied my face, trying to find something in it that would tell him he had a chance with me, but he had no chance and my face must have shown it, because at last he looked away, his face drawn, mournful, seeming ten years older now. 'I don't know,' he said, softly, more to himself than me. 'I don't know where I'll go now.'

'Come with me to see Doctor Cameron,' I said, knowing that wasn't what he'd meant but using the opportunity anyway.

He shook his head sadly, not looking at me. 'I'll have to think about things,' he said, still mostly to himself. 'I'll have to decide what to do.'

'I wish I could help you,' I said.

He lifted his eyes to mine. 'I want to be alone now,' he said. 'I'm sorry, I don't like to be rude, but I want to be alone to think about things.'

I considered. There was no way I could physically force him to come with me, and I was convinced I wasn't going to be able to talk him into giving himself up. But it might be best to leave him alone. There was no way out for him, and sooner or later he'd have to see it for himself. Since I was reasonably sure he wasn't a violent type, I thought it most likely that when he did see the situation was hopeless he'd quietly give himself up.

The thought touched my mind that he might also kill himself, if things seemed hopeless enough, but that I thought unlikely. He was a resourceful man, and though retiring he wasn't despairing, or at least he didn't seem despairing. In any case, I had no real choice.

So I said, 'All right, Dewey. I'll be in Doctor Cameron's office for five or ten minutes. Then I'm afraid we'll have to come looking for you.'

He nodded, his face mournful.

I got to my feet. 'I am sorry,' I said. 'But there's nothing I can do.'

'I know.'

'Thank you for the coffee,' I said.

He nodded, but he was distracted by the thoughts inside his own head.

I hesitated an instant longer, and then I left.

ELEVEN

Doctor Fredericks said, 'You left him there?'

'What else was I going to do?' I asked him. 'Grab him one-handed by the scruff of the neck and carry him here?'

Doctor Cameron said, 'Lorimer didn't mean anything, Mr. Tobin. There was nothing else you could have done.'

'The point is,' Doctor Fredericks said, 'you've got it into your head this man is innocent and you really don't want the hypothesis tested. If we had this Dewey character here in this room, it just might turn out he wasn't so one hundred per cent guiltless after all, and you don't want to take the chance of risking your professional pride.'

'I am on Dewey's side,' I admitted. 'The life he's worked out for himself is unorthodox, I grant you that, but it obviously works for him and it doesn't harm anybody else and I hate to be the one to spoil it all for him. Particularly when I am absolutely convinced he isn't the injurer. But I know there's no choice, you can't leave a stowaway at large once you've learned of his existence, you have to track him down and take a look at him and ask him questions, whether you believe he's done anything wrong or not. If there'd been any way for me to bring Dewey here from the kitchen, believe me I would have done it, if only to save myself the time and effort we're going to have to put into looking for him.'

Bob Gale said, 'Why don't we go back to the kitchen right now? Maybe he's still there.'

'Not a chance of it,' I said. 'Dewey is far from unintelligent. I guarantee you he left that kitchen thirty seconds after I did. At this very moment, I'm sure he's in whatever he considers his best hiding place, and he's sitting there praying we don't find him.'

'We will, of course,' Doctor Cameron said. 'The Midway is a finite structure, so we're bound to turn him up eventually.'

'We should start,' Doctor Fredericks said. 'The longer we stand around, the better chance he has to find a good hiding place.'

'He'll already know where he's going,' I said, 'and I imagine he's already there. But I agree we should get started, if only to end the suspense for Dewey as quickly as we can.'

78

Doctor Cameron said to me, 'The one problem, it seems to me, is searching occupied bedrooms.'

'He won't be in any,' I said. 'If we were to flush him, and he got away from us and was on the run, he might hide briefly in someone's room, but for now he'll be in some hiding place familiar to him.'

'I agree,' Doctor Fredericks said, and I looked at him in surprise. Whenever Fredericks agreed with anybody I was surprised. He said, 'From what Tobin has said of Dewey, now he'll want to be in a place he thinks of as home. His burrow, you might say.'

I said, 'Let's get going. I want to get this over with, too.'

Doctor Cameron said, 'Of course. The only question left is, who goes with who? Bob and Lorimer are the two most able-bodied among us, so one of us should be with each of them.'

Fredericks said, 'There should be a doctor with each team, so that would put Gale with you, Doctor, and Tobin with me.'

'Very good,' said Cameron, an opinion I didn't share, and we all got to our feet.

TWELVE

There was a central corridor running the length of the attic, with storage rooms on both sides of it, making it the simplest floor to search. Fredericks and I had come up the rear staircase and Doctor Cameron and Bob had come up the front – there being two staircases even up to this level – and we nodded and waved to one another down the length of the corridor, outlined for one another by the blue-gray light of dawn outside the windows at each end of the building.

It was well after five o'clock. We had started in the basement, keeping staircases always in sight, keeping each other almost always in sight, searching slowly and with care. We were all smudged and sooty by now, and none of us was in a good humor. Fredericks had become more and more savage in his needling of me, and I had turned mulish and sullen, to the point sometimes of hoping our quarry *would* evade us.

As apparently he had. We'd come up floor by floor, room by room, every room except those bedrooms currently occupied by residents, and we'd never found so much as a trace of Dewey's existence. We hadn't found any cache of his clothing, though tonight he'd worn a different shirt and sweater than he'd had on last night, and in any case if he was a permanent resident here, however subterranean, he would have to have a permanent corner in which to keep his possessions. But we hadn't found it.

Our method of search in the attic was typical of what we'd done on the floors below, but simpler. I stood in the hall, watching the doors and the staircase, while Fredericks entered each room in turn and thoroughly searched it. Down the other way, Doctor Cameron was the one on guard in the hall while Bob Gale did the searching.

We met at last in the middle. Bob was baffled and on the verge of becoming very angry, with the anger of someone who's had a practical joke played on him, and Doctor Cameron was looking put upon, almost petulant. With the dirt smudges on his face, and his general weariness, he no longer looked either distinguished or competent, and in fact he was reminding me of somebody, somebody from the past. Who?

J. Roger Urbermann! That's who it was, J. Roger Urbermann. About seven years ago that was. A hooker had offered to trade the location of a wanted man for her own freedom, and when we'd accepted the trade the name she'd come up with had been J. Roger Urbermann, of whom we'd never heard. Jock, my partner — how easy those words trip out — Jock was of the opinion she was making the whole thing up, having nothing to lose, but we checked the name anyway, and damned if it wasn't a real person, an absconding banker from Youngstown, Ohio, a fiftyish bank president who'd been draining off funds for years and who — in circularese — took flight to avoid prosecution once the truth was discovered. He was living in a residence hotel on Broadway and doing clerical work at one of those store-front places that do your income tax for you, and he'd made the mistake of befriending his neighbor at the hotel, who was our hooker. In a post-coital glow of warmth, he'd told her the truth about who he was. We picked him up at work and he tried to run away from us, but Jock tackled him and he rolled a bit in the gutter, and when he arose he was a grubby and defeated portly little man with only an echo remaining of the distinguished and self-confident banker he'd once been.

And Doctor Fredric Cameron, sooty and exhausted and petulant in the attic of The Midway, was an almost dead ringer for J. Roger Urbermann. All at once he seemed to me frail and unsure of himself and not really competent. A vague man, who had responded to his first real emergency at the halfway house he'd founded by running to New York to find someone else to be the 'expert'. Why wasn't *he* the expert? Wasn't the answer to this mess inside the brain of one of his residents. Wasn't it his *job* to look for answers inside those brains?

I knew these were unworthy thoughts even as I was thinking them, that they were the result of my own exhaustion and petulance, my frustration at not having found Dewey, and my aggravation at having spent the last hour alone with Doctor Lorimer Fredericks. But I also knew there was some portion of truth in them, that Doctor Cameron was not the incisive and confident man he appeared to be, that he was both more complex and less strong than that, and that at some level of complexity in his makeup there was a way in which he and Doctor Fredericks needed and complemented one another.

Doctor Fredericks was the first to speak when we all came together: 'We don't seem to have him.'

Bob Gale said, defensively, 'We *looked*, doggone it! He

didn't get through *us, we* were careful.'

'Everyone was careful,' I said. 'I'm sure he didn't get through anybody. He's simply found somewhere to hide that we haven't come across.'

Doctor Cameron said, 'We've searched the entire building, I vouch for that.'

Bob said, 'Not the bedrooms. I bet you somebody's hiding him. Maybe he's shacked up with one of the women. What we ought to do is roust everybody out and search their rooms.'

'Dewey's a loner,' I said. 'He won't be in anybody's room, he's got some hidden place of his own.'

'You know a lot about Dewey,' Fredericks said savagely. 'Everything but where he is.'

'He's somewhere inside this building,' I said. 'I'm sure of it.'

'Or inside your head,' Fredericks said.

Doctor Cameron raised a hand, vaguely. 'Lorimer, please.'

Fredericks turned on him. 'Has it ever occurred to you, Doctor,' he said, 'that this man could be making fools of us? This, this Dewey could be an invention of his own, for whatever his reasons. You know as well as I do he may be the least stable individual under this roof.'

I said, 'Don't you get tired of covering the same ground? Debby remembers meeting him, too, did you forget that?'

'Not at all,' he said. 'Debby remembers meeting him in March, over three months ago. *You're* the only one who claims to have seen him in the last two days. You can't go out of your room without meeting Dewey, but no one else has seen him at all.'

Doctor Cameron said, 'Lorimer, you're upset because we didn't find the man, but you can't seriously believe he doesn't exist. If he existed in March, surely he exists now.'

'Then why didn't we find him?'

Doctor Cameron shook his head. 'I don't know.'

I said, 'He has a hiding place we haven't found.'

Fredericks rounded on me. 'Where, goddamn it? You keep saying that, but where *is* this hiding place? In the fourth dimension? Is he a poltergeist? A familiar spirit? Do you see Dewey everywhere, Tobin, or just at The Midway?'

Bob Gale said, 'Doctor Fredericks, Mr. Tobin wouldn't lie about Dewey. I just bet you're going to find him in one of the residents' rooms.'

'I don't think so,' I said.

'Your disbelief,' Fredericks told me, 'is the strongest argument in the theory's favor.' He turned to Cameron. 'I suppose we'll have to look.'

Cameron was worried and vague. 'That would mean telling the residents what's going on,' he said. 'Just what I've been trying to avoid.'

Bob said, 'Tell them we saw a burglar, we're not sure whether he's still in the house or not.'

Fredericks nodded his approval. 'Very good,' he said.

I said, 'Bob and I shouldn't search with you, it would look odd.'

'We'll do better on our own,' Fredericks said.

I said, 'Doctor Cameron, when you're done with the search I'd like to speak to you in your office.'

'Of course,' he said.

'Alone.'

He frowned, and glanced at Fredericks, but then nodded and said, 'If you want.'

'In the meantime,' I said, 'I'll be in my room.'

I felt them watching me as I walked heavily down the corridor to the stairs.

THIRTEEN

I had fallen asleep again, and once more it was Bob Gale who woke me, shaking my shoulder and calling my name. I had been sleeping without dreams this time, and merely said, 'Thank you, Bob,' and sat up.

He said, 'Doctor Cameron says he's ready for you.' He seemed more subdued than before, and in some obscure way more guarded.

'Thank you,' I said. 'The search of the residents' rooms is done?'

'Yes.'

'He wasn't there.'

'No.'

I got up from the bed. I was already dressed, except for my shoes, which I now stepped into. 'I didn't think he would be,' I said.

Bob watched me in silence for thirty seconds or so, and then blurted, 'Doctor Fredericks thinks you're lying on purpose.'

I looked at him. 'Does he? Has he given me a motive?'

'To cover your failure, he says. He says you have a need for failure, ever since your partner got killed because you weren't with him, and you tend to invent complications to confuse people and distract them from your failures.'

'He told you about my partner, did he?'

Bob looked embarrassed. He nodded.

I said, 'What's his explanation for Debby having seen him?'

'He says you picked somebody who used to be here but left a few months ago, so there'd be people like Debby who'd remember him and seem to back up your story.'

'He invents some nice complications himself, Doctor Fredericks does,' I said. When Bob didn't respond to that, I looked at him and saw a deep frown creasing his forehead. I said, 'You believe him, Bob?'

'Nooo,' he said, as though the sentence should be longer than that.

I said, 'But what?'

'Nothing,' he said, and looked away from me.

'But what, Bob?'

He turned abruptly back. 'Doggone it, Mr. Tobin, we

searched! We looked everywhere, you know we did. Where the heck is he?'

'I don't know,' I said. 'I wish I did know, I'd like to have Doctor Fredericks off my back for a while.'

'That's why you want to see Doctor Cameron now, isn't it?'

'Yes. Let's go.'

We left the room and started down the hall toward the front staircase. Bob said, 'What are you going to tell him? I'm sorry, I shouldn't ask that.'

'I don't mind. I'm going to tell him he has to make a choice. Either Doctor Fredericks is kept completely away from me, either I'm allowed to do this job my own way without badgering and interference, or I'm leaving.'

'That's what they think you're going to say,' he said.

'I suppose it's fairly obvious.'

'Doctor Fredericks wants Doctor Cameron to let you go.'

'That was fairly obvious, too.'

'Doctor Cameron isn't sure whether he's going to ask you to stay or not.'

I glanced at Bob, saw his serious face, and nodded. J. Roger Urbermann. 'That wasn't quite as obvious,' I said, 'but it was a possibility.'

'I wish things could have gone better for you here,' he said. He was waving good-by to me already.

And it was all over a side-issue, that was the frustrating part of it. Dewey wasn't the injurer, I was convinced of that, but it was the existence of Dewey – the alleged existence of Dewey, Doctor Fredericks would say – that was fouling everything up, making it impossible for me to get on with the task I came up here to do.

Where was he? Where could he be? Somewhere in the house, I was certain of that, somewhere in the house. But where? We *had* searched everywhere, that was the devil of it. Fredericks had the evidence on his side.

We went down the broad front staircase to the truncated hall at the foot and turned toward Doctor Cameron's office. Ahead of me was the side entrance, the main entrance since whatever distant remodeling had removed the original main entrance at the foot of the front stairs. I had come in through that door down there less than forty-eight hours ago, and in that time I had done nothing—

Wait!

I stopped in my tracks, and Bob went on another step without me before he realized I was no longer moving. He looked back at me, saying, 'Mr. Tobin?' but I had no interest in explanations. I turned and hurried back the way we'd come.

Ahead of me was the staircase we'd come down, on the left. There was no door in the wall opposite it, the nearest one being seven or eight feet to this side. I came to that door, opened it, and stepped into a smallish parlor or waiting room, with a few old sofas and lamps about. This was one of the two rooms set aside for residents to entertain visitors in, if any. Visitors at The Midway were rare.

Bob had trailed along behind me, and stood in the doorway watching me prowl around the room. 'What is it, Mr. Tobin?'

'Nothing here,' I said, but not to him. I was mumbling to myself, absorbed in the thought that had occurred to me. I brushed past Bob, back out to the hall again, and hurried on down past the staircase to the next door on the right wall, which led me into a narrow room full of metal shelving. Paper and envelopes and other clerical supplies were stacked up here, and an ancient mimeograph machine stood inkily under the window opposite the door.

There was a door in the right-hand wall, which was the wall I was interested in. I opened it and found a closet with more supplies on the shelf, two old push-brooms leaning against the rear wall, and one black-and-red-check jacket hanging on a hook on the back of the door. I went into the closet, studying the walls in there, and Bob stood behind me, asking foolish questions.

It was Sheetrock, large square pieces of Sheetrock nailed to two-by-four framing, and no one had ever bothered to tape the lines where the pieces met. It was, after all, merely a closet in an obscure storeroom.

The center piece in the right wall. I tugged at it and it came tilting toward me, and in the darkness on the other side I heard a scuttling that could have been mice. 'Dewey!' I called, but there wasn't any answer.

I pulled the loose piece of Sheetrock away, and someone had fastened a rough handle to the other side, making it easier to fit into place from that side. I said over my shoulder. 'Bob, go get Doctor Cameron. Tell him I've found Dewey.'

'Yes!' he shouted, and dashed away.

FOURTEEN

'Dewey.'

There was no answer. And no more scuttling.

I wished I had a flashlight. It seemed impenetrably dark in there. I looked in, and I also wished I still had the same conviction in Dewey's essentially nonviolent nature.

Any animal will attack when cornered.

'Dewey.'

Not a sound.

'Dewey, why make us come in and get you? There'll just be scuffling, and everybody will feel embarrassed. Come on out, now. Doctor Cameron is coming, he wants to talk to you. He wants to help you figure out some better way to live. But a way you'll agree to, Dewey. I promise you, it'll be a way that you'll like, too. Dewey?'

Still nothing. Did he think at this point I could still be convinced he wasn't there?

Curiosity finally got the better of caution. I went down on my knees and warily leaned forward, putting my head through the opening just far enough so I could see inside.

It was about as I'd expected, a dead space left over at the time of the remodeling. It had looked like a fairly sloppy job, probably done by a do-it-yourself home handyman, and when people like that do major projects they never use plans, and the result is frequently odd leftover corners hidden away behind hasty walls. This one was about a foot and a half wide, and extended away to my left about ten feet.

And it was empty. I stuck my head in farther, I looked all around, and there was nobody there.

There was something to my left, a break in the wall past the end of the closet partition. I craned my neck, but could see nothing, and finally went on through the opening, moving on hand and knees, my broken right arm in its cast cumbersomely in my way.

I could stand inside, with two-by-four framework all around me. I edged down to the break in the partition and looked around the corner, and there was Dewey's home.

This space was much bigger, four feet wide and possibly a dozen feet long, with a rough stone wall at the far end, undoubtedly the new outer wall where the main entrance had originally been. Dim gray light seeped in from everywhere, cracks and chinks in walls and ceiling, and I could make out most of the details of Dewey's hidden room. There was a mattress on the floor down at the far end, with blankets neatly tucked in all around and two pillows in white cases leaning against the wall. Nearer, there was a wooden kitchen chair beside a wide shelf that had been attached to the two-by-fours on the side wall. Clothing hung from nails and hooks, and just to my left a small mirror dangled from a loop of wire nailed to a two-by-four. Some of the horizontal pieces in the wall framework had been used for bookshelves and to hold small personal items. There were also several candles around in different kinds of holders, none of them at the moment lit.

And the place was empty. It had the aura and feel of a lived-in room, but right now the owner was elsewhere.

Then what had that scuttling been, the sound I'd heard when I'd first pulled the piece of Sheetrock away? Perhaps it really had been mice after all.

No. Dewey was too neat, too fastidious a man. There would be no mice in this room, it was a human habitation no matter how much it was a place inside the walls. The scuttling had not been mice.

Was there another way out? I moved slowly along, studying the walls, poking at places that looked the slightest bit suspicious, but there was nothing. The only entrance seemed to be the one through which I'd entered.

Up? I looked up, and above me were the stringers, the two-by-twelve beams on which the upstairs floor was laid. I went over and got one of the candles, lit it, and by its light I began to study the ceiling.

And there it was. In the far corner, out of Dewey's living area entirely and down the opposite way from the closet entrance, the space between the last two stringers was empty, no flooring, nothing but a square of darkness. Far up through the hole the flickering candlelight hinted at more two-by-fours, the uncompleted inside of another wall. And down in front of me I could see the indentations and marks on the horizontal pieces of framework he used as his ladder.

'Mr. Tobin?'

Bob Gale's voice. I turned and called, 'Come in! Have you got a flashlight?'

His head appeared in the entrance at the other end of this

long narrow space. He blinked at me open-mouthed, then said, 'No. You want me to get one?'

'Never mind, you can use this candle. Come in, come in.'

I edged down to the break in the wall, the entrance to Dewey's bedroom, and waited impatiently for Bob to crawl through, get to his feet, and come sideways down to me. He looked past my shoulder at Dewey's room and said, 'Son of a gun!'

'Yes, isn't it? Did you bring Doctor Cameron with you?'

'Sure.'

Doctor Fredericks' voice said, 'Tobin?'

I looked over, and his disembodied head was jutting through the wall at knee-height, over there at the closet entrance. He looked foolish that way, and he was obviously aware of it, and I was delighted. I also felt savage joy at having been proved right, but I could wait to collect on that. I said, 'Fredericks, you go upstairs. You and Doctor Cameron. He'll be popping out up there somewhere.'

'What makes you think that?' He wanted to be argumentative again.

'Do what I say, you idiot,' I snapped at him. 'Argue with me later on. Now get upstairs.' I turned away from him and said, more quietly, 'Bob, there's a hole in the ceiling down at the far end. I can't get up there one-armed. Dewey went up there. Will you go up after him?'

'Sure!' He was happy as a boy allowed to play with the big kids.

'He won't fight you,' I said. 'At least, I don't think he will. But he'll try to run away.'

'I can hold him,' he said, full of confidence.

'All right. You go first, and I'll hand the candle up to you.' I looked back the other way, and Fredericks was gone. I could only hope he was doing what I'd told him.

Bob edged down to the far end of the narrow passage, and I followed him. He climbed up the framework quickly, and into the hole above, pausing at the last stage to reach down and take the candle from my upstretched hand. Then he went on up.

I called, 'See anything?'

'Narrow up here. Same as down there. It turns, down at the other end, I'll go take a look.'

'I'll go around and come up the stairs,' I called. 'Be gentle with him, if you can.'

'Okay.'

I turned away, hurrying sideways back to the closet entrance, crawling through, and stumbling to my feet inside. I left the closet and went through the storage room and out to the hall, where a couple of passing residents looked at me oddly. I knew I was probably sooty and sweaty again from crawling around between the walls, so not only were we out to capture the wrong person, but I was also more than likely in the process of blowing my cover here. How would we operate after this, to get the injurer? I had no idea.

I went up the front stairs, moving as quickly as I could, but before I was halfway I heard shouting up there, several people shouting, and Bob Gale's voice above them all, yelling, 'Stop! Stop!'

I lunged up the stairs, panting and gasping, and turned in the direction of all the noise, which abruptly stopped. Did they have him? I ran on, and ahead of me the corridor turned left. I trotted around the corner, and at the far end of the hall people were clustered at an open window, looking out, leaning forward and looking over one another's shoulders.

I came up to them, seeing Bob Gale and Doctor Fredericks in the front rank, both leaning out the window and looking down, with Doctor Cameron and Jerry Kanter and Robert O'Hara behind them, and William Merrivale and Marilyn Nazarro and Walter Stoddard making up a third row.

I stopped behind them, gasping for breath, and said, 'What happened?'

They didn't answer. They were immobile, like a piece of sculpture, or like worshippers at some strange shrine. Marilyn Nazarro, too short to see past the others' shoulders, was bobbing up and down, the only one of them in any kind of motion.

I said, 'Bob. What's the matter?'

Bob turned, his movement dislodging everyone else, breaking the spell that had been holding them all. He looked back, saw me, and drew his head in from the window. 'He's out here, Mr. Tobin,' he said, his voice and manner much more muted than usual.

Now the others turned to look at me, and moved back to give me room. Doctor Cameron said, 'We saw him go. He went out on the fire escape. We have wooden fire escapes, you know.'

I went into the space they'd cleared, and leaned to look out the window. At my elbow, Bob Gale said, 'It gave way.' I looked out.

There had been a wooden platform outside the window, constructed of wide planks, with two sets of steps leading from it, one up and the other down. Three of the planks now hung straight down against the rear wall of the house, leaving a hole in the platform nearly three feet wide.

Behind me, Doctor Cameron said, 'He was in a panic, of course, or he wouldn't have gone all the way through, he would have grabbed hold of the rail or some such thing. But he was too frightened and in too much of a hurry to think.'

I looked down through the hole, and down below there was blacktop between here and the garage. Lying face down on the blacktop, his arms and legs twisted in a shape vaguely reminiscent of a swastika, was Dewey, his head at an angle to his neck that is impossible in life.

Behind me, Bob Gale said, 'I kept shouting to him to stop, but he wouldn't.'

I drew back in and turned around, and they were all looking at me.

Doctor Fredericks said, 'So it seems you were right after all.'

I hit him in the mouth.

FIFTEEN

I had taken everybody completely by surprise, including myself. The swing had been awkward, since I'd only had the one hand to work with, but it had a lot of pent-up anger and frustration behind it, and all the weight of my rather stocky body, and it caught Fredericks flush on the mouth. He staggered backwards, eyes round with astonishment, arms pinwheeling, and I stumbled after him, not trying to hit him any more but just to regain my balance.

Bystanders kept us both from falling, and once I had myself both physically and emotionally under control again I turned to Doctor Cameron and said, 'We have to talk. In private.'

He was as shocked as Fredericks. 'After what you—'

I didn't have time for that. 'We have to talk,' I insisted. 'Before the police get here.'

The word *police* got through to him. He blinked and said, 'My God. Yes, you're right. In my office.'

'Good.' I turned to Bob Gale, saying, 'You go down and stand beside that body. Nobody is to move it, nobody is to come near it.'

'All right,' he said. He seemed stunned, whether by Dewey's death or my hitting Fredericks I didn't know.

I turned to Fredericks, whose upper lip was cut and bleeding. He was dabbing at it with a handkerchief and looking at me as though he still couldn't believe it had happened. I said, 'I'm sorry I did that. It was a momentary loss of emotional control.'

He nodded, continuing to watch me.

I told him, 'I want you to see to it that nobody leaves here and nobody makes any phone calls until the police arrive.'

He nodded again. 'I understand,' he said, his voice muffled by the handkerchief.

William Merrivale, the father-beater, said to me, 'Just who made you boss?' He was glowering at me, a look his father had probably gotten to know rather well.

I said, 'You'll find out what's going on as soon as everybody else does. Doctor Cameron, let's—'

Merrivale reached out and pushed my shoulder. 'I was talking to you.'

Doctor Cameron said to him, 'William, it's all right. We'll explain a little later.'

'Where does this guy get off socking people?'

'We don't have time for this,' I told Cameron.

'I know,' he said. 'William, be patient for just a little while. Mr. Tobin, shall we go?'

We went. Bob had already trotted away down the hall to take up his post beside the body, and now the rest of them followed Doctor Cameron and me toward the stairs. I could hear Merrivale back there, asking Fredericks insistent questions, and Fredericks answering in informationless monosyllables.

Neither of us said anything more until we were alone, and we weren't alone until we were actually inside his office. Then Doctor Cameron said, 'This is a terrible situation now.'

'Yes, it is,' I said, and sat down in the chair facing his desk.

He stayed on his feet, pacing around the office in aimless ovals. 'I suppose we have no choice,' he said gloomily. 'We have to call in the police now.'

'It's simpler than that,' I told him. 'In an accidental death under suspicious circumstances, which is what this is, the police come in whether we want them or not.'

'Now it's murder, isn't it?'

'Not exactly. In a court of law, it would be manslaughter. Of course if intent could be proved, then it would be murder. Among other things.'

He stopped and looked at me. 'What other things?'

'You and I are guilty of several crimes,' I told him. 'I don't know if you realize that.'

'No, I don't.' He wasn't sure whether to be offended or on the defensive, so he was a little of both.

I said, 'We have a number of rigged accidents, and we both know they're rigged accidents, and we don't report them to the authorities. Causing severe bodily damage, deliberately and maliciously, is a felony. In concealing our knowledge of a felony we have become accessories to the felony and equally guilty with the perpetrator.'

'But there were reasons—'

'I know the reasons. I doubt the local law will care about them. Particularly since this is potentially murder now, as you just pointed out. Because if this last accident is murder, an ambitious small-town D.A. might just try to turn the other accidents into attempted murders, and now we are not only accessories to attempted murder, but you and I, Doctor Cameron, are accessories before the fact to the actual murder of Dewey.'

He backed up to the sofa and sat down hard. 'My God,' he said. 'You take things that happen in life and reduce them to formulas of words and they completely change their character.'

'That's what the law is all about,' I told him. 'Getting the infinite variety of which human beings are capable broken down into a finite number of lowest common denominators. No defendant in the history of man ever recognized himself in court.'

Doctor Cameron said, dazedly, 'This is much much worse than I thought.'

'And there's another charge against me,' I said. 'I'm not licensed to act as a private investigator in this state, or in any state, but that's exactly what I was acting as here. You'd be an accessory to that, too, but I doubt anybody would concern themselves with you on that score – they'd already have you on a few more important matters. But me, with my past history, they'd gobble me up.'

Doctor Cameron shook his head, like a bull weary of the matador. 'What are we going to do?'

'What do you want to do?'

'I don't know,' he said. He spread his hands, and then looked at them, as though they should contain something helpful. 'Try to explain, I suppose,' he said.

'Throw ourselves on the mercy of the local authorities, in other words.'

'I don't see what else we can do.'

'After what you've told me about the local authorities,' I said, 'I can see only one result if we do that.'

He looked at me. 'What result?'

'Prison sentences for the both of us,' I told him. 'And for Doctor Fredericks as well. We could probably keep Bob Gale out of it, unless he insisted on dragging himself in, which he just might do.'

'Prison?' He stared around the room, as though it were disappearing. 'But – what would happen to The Midway?'

'I don't know. That isn't the point now, anyway. The question is what's going to happen to us.'

He blinked at me, frowning in heavy concentration. 'But what else can we do? The police will be coming whether we call them in or not. Could we keep them from finding out it's murder?'

'No. The injurer has been careless with saw marks before, and I'm sure he was this time, too. It will obviously be murder.'

'Could we pretend we didn't know any of the other accidents had been done on purpose?'

'Not any longer,' I said. 'My cover is blown now, no matter what we do at this point. Merrivale and the others who were with us upstairs know I'm not a regular resident now. They may not know who I am exactly, but they will know I'm a ringer. At least one of them will be bound to tell the police.'

'I see,' he said. 'And then the police will want to know just what you were investigating here.'

'Which would make things even worse than telling the truth in the first place.'

'Yes, it would.' He shook his head. 'I don't know,' he said. 'I have no experience in this sort of thing, I don't claim to be an expert in hiding things from the police—'

'Nobody's an expert at a situation like this,' I told him. 'Not you, and not me. We've got to work something out together.'

He looked at me. 'Do you have any ideas?'

'I'm not sure. I've been thinking of a couple of things, but I don't know if they'd work.'

'Such as what?'

'What if we didn't report it at all?' I asked him. 'What if we put the body in the garage until tomorrow? Then we could have a meeting of all the residents and explain what's going on, and ask them to help us by keeping their own mouths shut until tomorrow. That would give us one more day to try to find the injurer. If we could turn the murderer over to the police at the same time we turn over the body, it might keep them from poking too deep into what's going on here.'

He was shaking his head long before I finished, and when I was done talking he said, 'I'm sorry, but that would never work. You have twenty individuals out there, each with his or her own problems. In the first place, it wouldn't be fair to load this problem on top—'

'We really don't have the leisure,' I said, 'to think about what's fair and what isn't.'

'That isn't the most important objection,' he said. 'I can think of a good half-dozen of the residents who I guarantee you would not keep quiet if we asked them to. Merrivale, for one. Helen Dorsey. Molly Schweitzler. Phil Roche.'

95

'All right,' I said. 'You're right.'

'All we would succeed in doing—' he said, and the door opened and Fredericks came in. We both turned and looked at him.

His lip was no longer bleeding, but it looked puffy. There were vertical frown lines creasing his forehead, and his eyes had lost that look of absolute certainty which had always been one of the most infuriating things about him. He looked bewildered now, which made him seem much more human and bearable, and he was even tentative about coming in, saying, 'Am I intruding?'

Doctor Cameron looked at me to find out the answer, which I found embarrassing, and I hastily said, 'Of course not. We could use your help.'

He came in, shutting the door behind him, and said, 'Gale is standing over the body. Kanter and Debby Lattimore are watching the front door and the telephone. They seemed the most trustworthy for the job.'

Doctor Cameron said, 'It seems we have more of a problem than I thought, Lorimer. Come sit down.'

Fredericks sat on the sofa beside Cameron, who then told him what I'd outlined about our situation, and why we neither wanted to tell the local police the truth nor could we think of any satisfactory way of lying. He told Fredericks my wild stab of an idea to have all the residents lie for us and gave his objections to it, finishing, 'When you came in, I was just saying that all we would succeed in doing was getting those residents in trouble who did lie for us, and giving the others something extra to feel guilty about.'

'I can see it's no good,' I said. 'But I can't think of anything else.'

Fredericks said, 'We have to admit you aren't a bona fide resident, there isn't any choice in that any more. Merrivale and some of the others have already figured that much out for themselves.'

Cameron said, 'There's nothing to do but admit the truth and hope for the best.'

I said, 'There is no best if we tell the truth. Believe me, there's nothing but trouble for all three of us. We'll be a lot simpler for the local police to think about than the murderer, because they'll have us and they'll have to look for the murderer, and I doubt they'll be very good at it.'

Fredericks said, 'What if we claimed we hired you for some

other reason? We didn't know the accidents were planned, it was something else entirely that we wanted you for.'

Cameron, who was being totally fatalistic and defeatist now, said, 'What else could there be? All we have is the accidents.'

'We have Dewey,' Fredericks said. 'We could say we'd become aware that there was someone hiding in the building, living here who wasn't supposed to be, but we couldn't find him. That's what we hired you for.'

Cameron was delighted. 'That's brilliant, Lorimer! That would answer all the questions in a nutshell. Mr. Tobin, wouldn't that work?'

'Well,' I said, 'it gets you two off the hook, but it leaves me on, because it still has me performing as a private investigator without a license.'

Fredericks said, 'How serious is that?'

'They could jail me for it. It would be extreme, but they could if they wanted to. With my background, they might want to.'

'Would your background have to come out?'

'I imagine,' I said, 'they'll check into everybody's background, and particularly into mine, once they know I'm a plant.'

Cameron had the grace to say, 'That doesn't seem right. You shouldn't be left to face the music alone.'

Fredericks said, 'Psychic research? What about that? Ghosts and poltergeists, that sort of thing. You came up here to do some poltergeist research, and the poltergeist turned out to be Dewey. You don't have to be a licensed investigator to do psychic research, do you?'

'No, you don't,' I said, 'but I don't think we could make the story stand up. We three would be the only ones in the building to even mention poltergeists or anything like that. None of the residents would know of any manifestations, and it wouldn't take a very bright cop to begin to wonder why not.'

Fredericks grimaced. 'Oh, what a tangled web we weave,' he said.

Cameron said, 'What if you weren't taking money?'

I looked at him. 'I don't understand.'

'Well, you have to have a license to practice as a private detective, but doesn't that mean to be *employed* as a private detective?'

'I suppose so,' I said. I was dubious about where he was going with this idea.

He said, 'Then, if we weren't going to pay you, you wouldn't be breaking the law, would you?'

'Probably not. But why am I doing it for free?'

He spread his hands, glossing over the difficulty. 'You wanted to donate your time,' he said. 'We struck you as a worthy cause.'

'I don't think I'd be believed,' I said.

Fredericks said, 'What about barter?'

I said, 'A trade? What for what?'

'Your skill for ours,' he said. 'You say your background will come out in any case, so why not take advantage of it? Since your dismissal from the New York police force you've been despondent, can't work, so on and so on. We had this Dewey problem. You didn't feel that you wanted to commit yourself to an actual institution, and you couldn't afford private psychoanalysis, so when you heard about our stowaway problem you offered to come spend a month here and help us look for Dewey in return for our giving you what therapeutic help we could.'

I said, 'How did we find out about each other?'

Fredericks said, 'The same way you did in real life, through Detective Kengelberg.'

Cameron told me, 'A classmate of mine is Detective Kengelberg's cousin, and sent me on to him. Then he in turn sent me on to you. That's truly the way it happened.'

Fredericks said, 'Anything wrong with that?'

'I don't think so,' I admitted. 'It should have a plausible sound to it.'

'That's all we can hope for,' he said.

'It's more than I expected,' I told him. 'Doctor Fredericks, you have my respect. You're a clutch-hitter.'

He made a tight smile. 'I have my uses,' he said.

'And I apologize again for hitting you. I did it without thinking.'

'Naturally. If you'd thought you wouldn't have done it, I realize that.'

'I am sorry for it.'

He smiled again, more broadly, and touched a fingertip to his puffy lip. 'I found it very interesting,' he said.

I bet he did, at that.

SIXTEEN

Violent death brings things to a head. The echo inside The Midway had become a vibration, a tension, a hum. Faces looked paler and thinner, eyes were more prominent, bodies moved with a new awkwardness. Voices were more hushed.

And no one wanted to be alone. No general announcement had been made to the effect that the death of Dewey was classifiable as murder, but an aura of danger was nevertheless in the air, and people tended to flock together. It was lunch-time, so it was to the dining room that everybody gravitated, and no one wanted to be the first to leave.

I sat at a table with Bob Gale and Walter Stoddard and Jerry Kanter, we four being among the first arrivals, and I watched the room gradually fill up until everyone was present except Doris Brady, the culture-shock Peace Corps girl, and Nicholas Fike, the frail alcoholic. Neither of those two ever did come in for lunch that day.

But everyone else did. Robert O'Hara and William Merrivale, our two blond young football-player types, were at the table to my right. George Bartholomew and Donald Walburn, two of those already injured, were to my left at a table with Phil Roche and Edgar Jennings, two of the ping-pong players eliminated as suspects.

The room, in fact, had become sexually segregated, with three tables of men on one side of the room and three tables of women on the other side. Across from the table containing Bartholomew and Roche and Walburn and Jennings sat Debby Lattimore, with Marilyn Nazarro and Beth Tracy, Beth being another of the non-suspects from the ping-pong room. Across from my table was one seating Helen Dorsey, the compulsive housekeeper, along with Ruth Ehrengart and Ivy Pollett, my last two suspects, both of whom I was seeing for the first time. All I could say was that they both looked appropriate to their dossiers, Ruth Ehrengart a thin and washed-out woman who looked like someone who'd had a nervous breakdown after the birth of her tenth child, and Ivy Pollett also thin, but dryer, chalkier, the right appearance for a fortyish spinster who'd devoted her life to an ailing mother and, after the mother's death, gradually built up a many-faceted persecution complex involving attempted rapes and counterspies and all sorts of obscure plots. Was either of those two guilty of murder? Had Ivy Pollett, for instance, started to believe in the plots and the persecution again and had she started laying traps for her enemies?

But that kind of theorizing was no good. As I'd already seen in the past, a workable irrational motive could be developed out of the dossier of anyone in this room. That wasn't the way I was going to find the murderer. If I ever did find him.

Jerry Kanter rapped his knuckles softly on the table to get my attention, and gave a meaningful nod of his head. 'Look at that.'

He had meant the last table, across the way and to the right, where Rose Ackerson and Molly Schweitzler, whose accident had been the first round in this war, were sitting by themselves. I looked over there, and Rose was spoon-feeding Molly her lunch. Rose wore an expression of pleasurable concern, and Molly looked like a mournful child. Since Rose's mental problems had started when she had kidnapped a baby in her desperation for a substitute for her own grown-up and departed children, and since Molly was a woman with a record of gross and compulsive overeating when emotionally upset, it was not the healthiest sight in the dining room. But it was only the most blatant sign of what was going on at all the tables. There wasn't a person in this room, except for me, who hadn't emerged from a mental hospital at some time within the last four or five months. The aura that had overtaken The Midway, the new feel of the place rather than any specific threat or danger, was unsettling these people in disturbing ways. Hard-won victories were being recontested inside every brain in the room.

Jerry Kanter himself was another example. He watched Rose Ackerson feeding Molly Schweitzler her lunch, and he thought it was funny. A kind of savage pleasure had taken hold of him, and he couldn't have looked away if he'd wanted to. 'Isn't that the damnedest thing you ever saw?' he said. 'Just look at those two.'

'I see them,' I said, and looked away. I was more interested in watching those still on my suspect list.

Ethel Hall, for instance. She was serving as waitress at this meal, and her nervousness was so intense it was a miracle she hadn't yet dropped any of the plates she was carrying. She would talk to no one, meet no one's eye. She was the figure of fun, the lesbian librarian, and there was a certain amount of high-strung nervousness in her background. Was it the atmosphere in here today that was making her so jittery, or was she the injurer and was it the knowledge she was now a murderess that had unstrung her?

Or the two young men at the table to my right, Merrivale and O'Hara. They both had chips on their shoulders now, they were silent with one another; it was perfectly obvious that if either of them said a word, the other one would be at his throat. It wasn't that they were angry at one another – they were like nervous lions in a cage, who take out their upset by attacking one another. Both from time to time spent a few seconds glaring at me, Merrivale in particular, and I doubted I would manage to leave The Midway without Merrivale making at least one attempt to settle scores with me.

There was more nervousness across the way, where the two faces new to me, Ruth Ehrengart and Ivy Pollett, sat with hunched shoulders and downcast eyes, flanking Helen Dorsey, who looked grim and strained, her cheekbones prominent, her movements stiff and precise.

And finally, among my suspects present – Doris Brady and Nicholas Fike being technically suspects and both absent – was Debby Lattimore, at the table across the way and to the left. She and Marilyn Nazarro and Beth Tracy, the other two young ladies at that table, all looked silently terrified, with that look people have when they half believe something horrible is just behind them. Debby kept looking around, darting quick looks at the other tables and then turning hastily away whenever she chanced to meet someone else's eye.

Walter Stoddard – a suspect too, and at my table, facing me – said, 'What exactly are you, Tobin?'

I looked away from Debby and saw him studying me. He had a brooding expression on his face today, more thoughtful and less hopeless than I'd seen there before. I said, 'How do you mean?'

'Everybody knows you aren't kosher,' he said. 'But nobody knows what you are.'

I said, 'I'm a friend of a friend of Doctor Cameron.'

'You weren't at Revo Hill?'

I shook my head.

Jerry Kanter reluctantly gave up his study of Rose Ackerson and Molly Schweitzler. 'So you are a ringer.' he said. 'A counterspy. What are you, a cop?'

'No. I used to be on the force in New York City, but I haven't been for the last three years.'

Walter Stoddard said, 'Now you're a private detective?'

'No. In a way, I'm not really a ringer at all. I'm a kind of a mental patient, in fact. I don't want to go into that part of it.'

'Nobody's asking you to go into that part of it.' Stoddard said. 'All I asked you is what you're doing here.'

I was glad for the opportunity to try out the story on an audience that would be at least as wary, and probably more knowing, than the local police. Bob Gale, sitting now at my right, had been filled in by Doctor Cameron before lunch, and knew that officially he no longer had any part in anything that had taken place. I hoped he could remember that, and wouldn't try to add imaginative details while I was answering Stoddard.

But he was good. He maybe overplayed the 'isn't-that-interesting?' expression on his face, but neither Stoddard nor Jerry Kanter was likely to notice. They were devoting their full attention to me.

I said, 'I'm here on a kind of swap basis. Doctor Cameron suspected there was someone unauthorized living here, a kind of stowaway, and he didn't know what to do about it. He didn't want to call in the police to make a search, because he thought that might have a bad effect on some of the residents. His own searches hadn't come up with anything at all. He told the problem to a friend of his, a classmate from his college days, and the classmate sent him on to a cousin of his named Marty Kengelberg, a detective on the New York force. Marty knew me, and knew about my personal problems, and knew I'd been wanting some sort of psychiatric counseling, but I couldn't afford a regular psychiatrist, and I was damned if I was going to commit myself to an institution, so it looked as though I wasn't going to get helped. Marty brought Doctor Cameron and me together, and we offered to try to help each other out. I'd come here as a regular resident and try to find the stowaway, and he would give me personal sessions to see if he could help me in any way.' I spread my hands. 'So that's what I'm doing here. Looking for psychiatric help, and looking for Dewey.'

Stoddard had been watching me closely all the while I talked, and I wasn't at all sure he was going along with it, but it was Jerry Kanter who raised the first question, saying, 'How come you poked Doctor Fredericks in the eye?'

'I poked him in the mouth,' I said. 'And the reason I did it was because I was mad at him.'

'I figured that much,' Kanter said. 'The question is, why were you mad at him?'

'He made Dewey run,' I said. 'I knew Dewey would be scared, and I wanted us to come at him carefully. Fredericks was always against that, he just wanted to shout Dewey out of the house.'

Kanter grinned sidelong and said, 'That sounds like Fredericks, all right. He isn't happy if he isn't giving somebody a bad time.'

'I blamed Fredericks for Dewey going into a panic and falling,' I said. 'I think now it was unfair to blame him, but at the time I did.'

Stoddard said, 'Have they identified this Dewey?'

'Yes. Doctor Cameron went out and looked at the body and recognized him right away. His name was DeWitt, Frank DeWitt. He was one of the first residents ever to stay here, when The Midway opened six or seven years ago. Doctor Cameron says he remembers Dewey — DeWitt, I mean — he remembers DeWitt made a lot of fuss about leaving, said he wasn't ready for the outside world, but he didn't think much of it. A lot of residents feel that way, that's why there's the automatic six-month cutoff period, to keep people from getting too emotionally involved with this place. But Dewey wouldn't wean.'

Stoddard said, 'You mean he's been living here for six years? And nobody knew it?'

'That's right. There's little odd corners and false walls here and there in this building, and that's where he lived. Doctor Cameron tells me this house is over eighty years old, and it's been redesigned inside at least three times that he knows of. Nobody ever did any secret compartments or hidden passageways on purpose, they just naturally developed. Dewey found them, and fixed them up as living quarters.'

Bob, who hadn't been present for my conversation with Cameron, said, 'How come he called himself Dewey? So nobody'd know who he really was?'

'Probably it was partly that. Doctor Cameron looked into the old records, and it turns out DeWitt was brought up in an orphanage in New England, and his nickname there was Dewey. From the similarity of his own name and something to do with either the Admiral or the Governor, I suppose.'

Bob said, 'Or the decimal system, maybe.'

'Maybe.'

Kanter leaned closer and said, 'I've heard it doesn't look like an accident, you know.'

I said, 'Where did you hear that?'

'Around,' he said. 'Everybody knows it.'

Stoddard said, 'Do you mean there's nothing to it, Mr. Tobin?'

I looked at him, and I knew his belief in my story hinged on what I said right now. If I plumped for the accident theory, he'd never believe any of the rest of what I'd told him. If I said something that sounded like the truth, he might go along with the rest.

Bob Gale almost spoiled it all by saying, 'How could there be anything to it? He went out on the fire escape and fell, that's all.'

Jerry Kanter said, 'The platform broke, Bob, don't tell me. I was there.'

I said, 'There's a good chance it was tampered with. The police will check that out, that isn't up to me.'

Stoddard said, wearily, 'Then someone here must have done the tampering, is that it?'

'Probably,' I said.

'And the other accidents? Your arm, and Kay Prendergast hitting her head, and all the others?'

'If the platform was tampered with,' I said, 'then probably some or all of the other accidents were the result of tampering, too.'

Stoddard said, 'The police will want to question everybody, won't they? They'll suspect everybody here.'

'They'll have to.'

He looked around, frowning and worried. 'That won't be good for these people,' he said. 'That won't be good for any of them.'

'It's out of our hands now,' I said. 'When it's a question of murder, it's up to the police to do what they have to do.'

'But the murder,' Stoddard said. 'That really *was* an accident, wasn't it? Whoever has been doing this, they haven't been trying to kill anybody, have they? Just hurt them somehow.'

'I don't think the injurer particularly cares,' I said. 'If my accident was arranged, it was a very dangerous one. People have died before after falling down a full flight of stairs. And Kay Prendergast could easily have been killed by her head hitting that radiator. It's true, if Dewey hadn't been in a panic he probably wouldn't have been killed when that platform gave way, but the point is, a fire escape is something that you would normally use in a panicky situation anyway. And in any case, it isn't all that easy to find the right line between doing someone serious injury and actually killing him. The injurer has been lucky up till now, that's all.'

'We're twenty-some people here,' Stoddard said. 'Only one is a murderer.'

I said, 'If that one were to stand up and confess, it would make things a lot easier for everybody. But that isn't likely, and failing that, the police will have to treat this like any other murder investigation.'

Stoddard leaned closer to me. 'Do you have any influence with the local police?'

'None. In fact, I'll be very lucky if I'm not in serious trouble with them. What I've been doing comes very close to operating as a private detective without a license.'

'Not if you haven't taken any money for your work,' Bob Gale said. It was said a little too promptly, and with a little too blatant a look of ingenuousness, but neither Stoddard nor Kanter seemed to notice.

In answer to it, I said, 'I hope you're right, Bob. We'll just have to wait and see what the police have to say.'

Kanter said, 'What are they doing, anyway? The last I saw, there was one young cop out back by the body, and that was it.'

Bob said. 'There was a truck came in just before I came in here for lunch. It said something about State Police Mobile Lab on the side.'

Stoddard said, 'State Police? Won't the Municipal Police be investigating this?'

I told him, 'Smaller communities tend to use the state's technical equipment, rather than try to buy a lot of expensive stuff themselves that they won't be using more than once or twice a year.'

'But the local police,' he said, 'will do the actual investigation. Or will we all be questioned by people from the State Police?'

'Municipal,' I said.

'It might be better for everybody if the State Police did take over,' he said. 'They might be more understanding of the situation here.'

'The local yokels,' Kanter said, with a touch of defiance in his voice, 'can't stand the whole idea of us.'

'It's awful,' Stoddard said. 'It's awful to think of these people being questioned by policemen who don't understand them and who even hate them. It's going to drive some of these people right back inside.'

'Not me,' Kanter said. 'If there's one thing I've learned, it's not to let things get to me. That's something you still need to work on, Walter.'

Stoddard closed his eyes, and slowly shook his head.

Bob, trying to rush us all past an awkward moment, said, 'Maybe the person who did it will confess. He didn't really want to kill anybody, he just wanted to hurt people. Maybe this will shake him up, and he'll confess.'

'That'll be the day,' Kanter said, and something crashed to our right.

It was O'Hara and Merrivale. The tension had cracked between them and one or both had made the final move, and all at once they were half on their feet, half falling over the table, wrestling one another in grim silent fury, both red-faced and murderous, but too evenly matched for either to do much damage right away.

They'd knocked a chair over in lunging at one another, attracting everybody's eye, and now two or three of the women in the room screamed, giving in to their own method of relieving tension; when O'Hara and Merrivale toppled over and crashed onto the table, which gave way and tumbled them to the floor, the screams redoubled.

O'Hara and Merrivale rolled and struggled on the floor. Bob Gale and Jerry Kanter both made movements in their direction, as though to try to stop them, but I grabbed their arms to hold them back. 'Leave them alone,' I said, and had to shout it over the screams, which just kept getting louder.

Then the dining-room door was flung open, crashing into the wall, and three men came running into the room. The two in the lead were both in police uniform, and were both from the same mold as O'Hara and Merrivale, young beefy blond all-American types with permanently sullen expressions. Behind them came an older man, about forty-five, medium height, stocky, somewhat jowly about the face but not really fat. He was wearing a wrinkled brown suit, a thin white shirt and a narrow tan tie, and he was frowning with outrage.

It was the man in the brown suit who spoke, his voice

cutting across the screaming and the scuffling and everything else: 'Stop those two!'

The two in uniform stopped them. They ran to the two boys rolling and struggling on the floor and bent over them to whale away with nightsticks, all done quickly but methodically, the arms and the dark wooden sticks rising and falling almost in unison, the two policemen's faces showing nothing but absorption in the physical fact of what they were doing.

'Good God!' Stoddard cried, and before I could stop him he was on his feet and running over to try to clutch at the nightsticks and keep them from falling anymore.

He was shoved away with more distraction than irritation, and fell backwards into the table where Rose Ackerson and Molly Schweitzler were huddled together. All the screaming had stopped now, and everyone merely watched in stupefaction. Rose and Molly made frightened squeaks when Stoddard fell against their table, the sounds surprisingly loud in the new silence.

Stoddard fell heavily to the floor, and started at once to get up again, but the beating abruptly stopped and the two policemen rose from their bent-over positions, each now clutching one of the two young men by the forearm, dragging them to their feet.

They looked dreadful. Both were cut in various places on their heads, with thin straggly lines of blood running down over their foreheads and past their ears. O'Hara's mouth looked mashed and bloody, and so did Merrivale's nose. Both were dazed and only half-conscious, and neither put up any struggle as they were led shambling from the room.

We watched them go. Stoddard got himself clumsily to his feet and stood leaning against Rose and Molly's table, watching, his expression combining unbelief with the grimmest kind of fatalism.

When the two policemen had left the room, taking O'Hara and Merrivale with them, the man in the brown suit looked around at us, glaring as though to say he knew we were all in a plot together but that he would ferret it out, and then he called, 'Which one is Tobin?'

I got to my feet, feeling suddenly very nervous, very frightened. My stomach was getting small cramps, and a hard ball of nervousness had formed just up under the front of my rib cage. I said, 'I'm' – but it came out falsetto, a stupidly comical note. I cleared my throat and said, 'I'm Tobin.'

He looked at me. 'They all here, Tobin?'

'All but two,' I said.

'Go get them,' he told me. 'I want everybody to stay right here until they're called. Go get them and tell them that, Tobin, and when you've got them here come down to Cameron's office. I want to talk to you first.'

'I don't know which rooms they have,' I said.

'Then take somebody with you who does.'

Bob Gale popped up at once, saying, 'I'll come with you.'

I glanced at him, wishing he'd had sense enough not to draw attention to himself, but there was nothing to do but nod and say, 'All right.'

'Make it fast,' the man in brown said, and left the dining room, slamming the door behind him.

SEVENTEEN

Walter Stoddard came shakily over to the table and leaned with both hands on the back of his chair. 'So that's what they're going to be like,' he said.

'We shouldn't judge too quickly,' I said, but I could hear the lack of enthusiasm in my voice. What we had just seen was as shoddy a piece of police procedure as I'd ever heard of. There was no mark on either O'Hara or Merrivale that they'd given to one another. The police work in that instance had not only served to create injuries where there had been none, but in one stroke it had prejudiced every potential witness in the larger matter, the investigation of a murder.

And somehow I could feel the prejudice extending to me. I had not chosen to be the man in the brown suit's emissary to get Doris Brady and Nicholas Fike, but I was his emissary, and everyone knew by now that I was in some obscure way a near-policeman myself, and all at once I was a representative of the enemy camp.

But I was in neither camp, really. The man in the brown suit would no more accept me as a policeman than these people would accept me as a resident. I was a wax apple in both bowls.

Bob Gale said, 'We ought to get going, Mitch.' He still didn't have sense enough to put a clearly defined distance between us, which could eventually cost him dearly.

I nodded to him, and said to Stoddard, 'We can only hope for the best.' He gave me a bleak look without answering, and I reluctantly turned away from the table.

Bob and I walked to the door, and I could feel the eyes on us. You could almost smell the fear in the room now. There would be more than one case of hysterics in here before the day was over.

A uniformed policeman was on guard just outside the door. He was neither of the two who'd been in the dining room, but was a big rangy boy with red hair showing beneath his uniform cap. His face was rural, open, amiable, perhaps gullible. He was the one who had stood guard over Dewey's body until his superiors and the State Mobile Lab showed up. He looked at us and his eyes were odd, white-rimmed, and it took me a second to realize that he too was frightened and was showing his fear with his eyes, the way horses do.

Of course. This was The Midway, and we were the residents, and to the local people the residents of The Midway were all lunatics. A whole house full of crazy people, that's what it seemed like to them. And here was this boy, no more than twenty-five, standing guard over a door, an unlocked door, with twenty crazy people just on the other side.

I said to him, softly, to reassure him, 'I'm Tobin. I've been sent to get the other two residents.'

'Yes, sir,' he said, and relaxed a little bit, but not much. 'Captain Yoncker told me,' he said. He was not looking at Bob Gale at all, preferring to concentrate his attention on someone – me – who was supposed to be reasonably sane.

Bob and I walked on past him, and after that I let Bob lead the way. We headed in a direction that I knew was toward the rear staircase, and after we rounded the first turn Bob said, in an excited whisper, 'What are we going to do, Mitch?'

'We're going to get Doris Brady and Nicholas Fike,' I told him.

'I don't mean that. We've got to do something about these cops! They aren't going to find the killer, you know that. All they're going to do is give everybody a bad time.'

'It isn't up to us to try to stop them,' I said, 'and I imagine we'd both get ourselves in a lot of trouble if we tried. I'll speak to Doctor Cameron about what happened to O'Hara and Merrivale, but after that it's up to him. It really is, Bob. You and I could only make things worse.'

'What if we found the killer ourselves?' he asked me. He was excited and intent, and he thought he was making perfect sense. 'Turn the killer over to that Captain Whatsisname—'

'Yoncker, the officer said,' I told him. 'Captain Yoncker.'

'If we turn the killer over to Captain Yoncker,' Bob said intently, 'he won't have any excuse to hang around here anymore.'

'We don't know who the killer is,' I pointed out. 'And Bob, we can't do any poking around with this house full of Yoncker's police. He wouldn't like it.'

'We could *try*.'

'No.'

'You mean you won't? I don't see how you can be like that! Didn't you see what they did to—'

'I saw it,' I said. 'I have more experience than you, Bob, so

110

let me tell you something. The only sensible thing to do when men like that are around is be very small and very quiet and hope they don't notice you. And if they do notice you, you get even smaller and quieter. You don't annoy them, Bob, because they have all the power, all the authority and all the safety they need. There's nothing you can do to them, and a lot they can do to you, and you'd better start acting as though you understood that.'

We'd reached the rear stairs, and started up them. Bob looked mutinous and disappointed in me. 'I'd thought you were a different kind of guy,' he said.

'I'm sorry,' I said.

We went on up the stairs, and he silently pointed that we were to turn right, away from my own room and the area I knew best. We had nothing more to say to one another, both correctly understanding that we had reached a point where true communication between us was impossible, until Bob stopped and pointed to a door on the right, saying, 'This is Fike's room.'

I rapped on the door, and called Fike's name, and nothing happened. I knocked again, and still nothing happened, so I turned the knob and pushed the door open and went in.

The room was empty. It was a smaller room than mine, but very similar in furnishings and appearance. Two drawers of the metal bureau stood half-open, and when I went over to look they both contained personal items of Fike's but not very many. Both drawers were well under half-full.

'Maybe he's in the bathroom,' Bob said.

'Go take a look,' I told him.

He left, and I went over to the closet and opened the door. There were a few things hanging in there, a topcoat and a suit and a couple of shirts and two pairs of trousers, but they were to both sides, leaving the center of the rod empty except for some wire and wood hangers. There was nothing on the shelf except a gray hat tucked off to the side.

I went over to the window, which faced the same side as my room. A green wall of leafy tree branches obscured the view. The window was open. I leaned out and looked down. There was an ornamental line of stone jutting out about four feet below the bottom of the window, a space too narrow to be a ledge. The ground ten-to-twelve feet below that was soft dark loam, shadowed by the trees.

I heard a sound behind me. and brought my head in again.

Turning, I saw Bob in the doorway. He said, 'He wasn't there.'

'He's run away,' I said. 'Packed a suitcase and went out the window.'

Bob looked around in surprise. 'You sure?'

'Positive.'

'You mean, he's the one?'

'I doubt it. Pressure made him run, not guilt. Our injurer has had lots of time to get used to pressure, he's injured people six other times before Dewey was killed.'

Bob came over to the window and looked out, but there was nothing to see but leaves and branches. 'Where's he going to go? He's got no place to go.'

'I imagine,' I said, 'he'll be picked up in a bar somewhere in Kendrick.'

He looked at me. 'That's really rotten,' he said. 'He came here because he needed things quiet. We all did. This is really rotten, Mr. Tobin, it's rotten rotten rotten!'

He was getting too excited, and for the first time I was forcibly reminded of the dossier on him. Vietnam had been rotten too, and he'd come out of it so full of anguish it had taken three years in a VA hospital to undo one year of Vietnam. I didn't want him breaking down now, mostly because I had the feeling he would tend to break in the direction of thrusting himself toward martyrdom. I had no doubt but that Captain Yoncker and his men were prepared to gobble up any martyrs they were given.

I said, 'Fike will be all right. As all right as he would have been anyway. Come on, let's see Doris Brady.'

He was reluctant to leave the room, though there was nothing either of us could do there. I had to go over to the door and stand there, and finally he came along.

Doris Brady's room was around one more corner, and once again I knocked and received no answer. Bob looked wonderingly at me and said, 'Her, too?'

'I shouldn't think so,' I said. 'She's a different type.' I knocked on her door again, and called her name, and at last pushed open the door.

Empty. I walked into a room that seemed no more feminine than my own or the one Fike had occupied, except for the shoes under the bed. There were no drawers pulled open in the metal bureau here, and the window, which faced the road side of the house, was shut.

'Would she use the same bathroom as Fike?' I asked.

'Sure. It's just down the hall. It was empty when I looked.'

I went over to the closet and opened the door. On the shelf was a suitcase. The clothing was sparse hanging from the rod, but it was evenly spaced.

I was about to shut the door again when I sensed the eyes. I looked down and to my right, and started despite myself.

She was sitting on the floor, knees tucked-up under chin, arms wrapped around legs, back against the side wall of the closet. And she was staring at me, solemnly and unblinkingly. I looked back at her, and somehow I had the feeling she wasn't really seeing me at all, though when I moved my head her eyes tracked, following me. But they weren't like living eyes at all, they were like the eyes in a painting that are looking at you wherever you stand in the room.

I said, 'Doris.' There was no change in her expression, no response at all. I heard Bob moving in my direction, and waved him away with a hand behind my back. 'Doris,' I said again, and her eyes didn't even flicker. I knew it was hopeless to try to reach her, but I said, 'Will you come out now, Doris?' No response.

I backed away from the closet, leaving its door open, and when I was out of her range of vision I turned and said to Bob, 'Go get Doctor Cameron.'

'What is she—? Is she—?'

'Go get Doctor Cameron!'

He left.

EIGHTEEN

The first man through the door was Yoncker, and I felt a tightening in my chest, because I knew that no matter how practical I had been with Bob Gale, I would not now be able to stop myself from trying to protect Doris Brady from this man. I stood there braced for the worst, and then Doctor Cameron came into the room behind Yoncker, and I suddenly realized I'd been holding my breath. I exhaled, and Doctor Fredericks came in, and then the two policemen who'd beaten up O'Hara and Merrivale.

Yoncker said to me, brusquely, 'Where is she?'

I treated the question as though it had come from Doctor Cameron, and looked at him as I made my answer. 'She's in the closet, Doctor. Sitting on the floor, on the right.'

Yoncker started for the closet, but Doctor Cameron got there first, and I heard Cameron's voice start, soft and reassuring. Yoncker, standing behind him and trying to see past him, said, 'We can get her out of there, Doctor, and then you'll be able to talk to her.'

Fredericks said, 'That won't be necessary.' His tone was even colder than usual, and I looked at him in some surprise, to see him considering Captain Yoncker with undisguised repugnance. 'Doctor Cameron knows what is best in this situation,' he added, and turned to me to say, 'Did you talk with her at all?'

'I spoke her name two or three times,' I said. 'And asked her if she'd like to come out now. I didn't get any response at all.'

Yoncker, frustrated with the girl in the closet, shouldered between Fredericks and me to say, 'What about the other one?'

'Gone,' I said, and described what I'd found.

Yoncker was pleased, given a situation he recognized. 'Flew the coop, eh? Admission of guilt, do you suppose?'

Fredericks answered him, saying, 'Not at all. Fike has a history of alcoholism; emotional upset tends to drive him back to the bottle. You'll find him in the nearest bar.'

'But it could still be guilt,' Yoncker insisted.

'Nicholas Fike,' Fredericks said with really blatant contempt, 'doesn't have the nerves to set a mousetrap. He's not the man you want, if it's the guilty party you're looking for.'

'Of course it is,' Yoncker said. He was honestly baffled. 'What else would I be here for?' He actually hadn't understood Fredericks' half-accusation that he would be willing to railroad the first handy suspect he found, and I wondered if Fredericks would repeat it in even more obvious terms.

But he didn't. He merely shrugged, and turned away, going over to Doctor Cameron. The two of them murmured together in the closet doorway, and then Fredericks turned back to Yoncker and said, 'It would be best to leave Doctor Cameron alone with the young lady.'

'I could leave somebody here on guard,' Yoncker offered, 'if you think it's a good idea.'

'It's a rotten idea,' Fredericks told him. 'There's only one terrified girl in that closet, not a tiger escaped from the zoo.'

Yoncker was reluctant to leave, but then his eye lit on me again and he said, 'All right, Tobin, you and me can spend the time getting to know one another. Come on along.'

We all left the room except Doctor Cameron, who remained in the closet doorway, talking softly to the girl sitting in there on the floor. We other five – Yoncker and Fredericks and the two policemen and me – went to the front stairway and down to the first floor, where Fredericks said, 'Do you need me right now?'

'Not for a few minutes,' Yoncker said. It was obvious he disliked Fredericks as much as Fredericks disliked him, but he hadn't decided yet whether Fredericks was powerless or not. He said, 'Where you going to be, in case I need you?'

'In the dining room.'

Yoncker wasn't too happy about that. He didn't want Fredericks messing around with his suspects, I could see that in Yoncker's eyes and his stance and the way he moved his head. But there was no legitimate objection he could think of to make, so he gave a graceless shrug of the shoulders and said to me, 'Come along, Tobin.'

He led me to Doctor Cameron's office, where the two uniformed policemen waited outside. Yoncker and I went inside, and he pointed to the chair in front of Cameron's desk, saying, 'Sit there.' I did so, and he himself settled into the chair behind the desk. He rested his elbows on the blotter, leaned his head forward, and said, 'Tell me about all this.'

I told him the story, and he listened without interruption. In some ways I was sure he was a fool, but in other ways I was just as sure he wasn't, and I knew he was mentally testing every element of the story as I gave it to him, looking for weaknesses in the fabric, inconsistencies, any indication of falsehood.

I hated to be lying. My training and history and inclination were all opposed to it. I had been on the force too long to ever be really comfortable pitted against a policeman. So I had to keep reminding myself what sort of man this was, and what the result would be if I were to tell him the complete and open truth.

When I was done, he sat there and studied me a few seconds. and then said, 'I'll check all that, you know.'

'Of course,' I said.

'You want to tell me what you got bounced for, or would you rather I got it from New York?'

'I'd rather you got it from New York.'

He gave a little smile, as though we were fallen angels together, and said, 'Bad stuff, huh? Shook you up.'

'Yes.'

'You figure this'd help?' He gestured with his head, a movement implying not merely the room we were in but the whole building. 'Being locked up with a lot of loonies, that's supposed to get you back on your feet?'

'They're not loonies.'

'You been listening to that doctor. They're loonies, all right.' He nodded, agreeing with himself. 'That arm of yours,' he said. 'What happened to it?'

'I fell down a flight of stairs, the first day I was here.'

'Fell, or was pushed?'

'I fell, so far as I know, I was alone.'

'You know what we've got here is murder,' he said. 'You know those boards on the fire escape were half sawn through.'

'I thought it might be something like that,' I said.

'There've been a lot of accidents around here,' he said. 'Two of these loonies are up in Memorial Hospital.'

'I know. One of them was hurt just yesterday.'

'Hit her head.' He chuckled, and said, 'You wouldn't think that would bother these people, would you? A hit on the head.' He sat back and said, 'You used to be a big-city cop, Tobin, how come you're so stupid?'

I didn't know what he meant, and that paralyzed me. I was vulnerable in so many directions at once that I didn't know which way was a safe response, so all I could do was blink at him and say, 'Stupid? Am I? I don't know what you mean.'

'I mean,' he said, 'what I mean is, there's been all these accidents. You had one yourself. You're an ex-cop, you're from New York City, you're supposed to be bright, you're supposed to be a lot brighter than us country cops, Tobin, but it never occurred to you those accidents might not be accidents at all. Is that right, Tobin?'

'There've only been two since I got here,' I said. 'Me and the Prendergast girl. If I'd been here for all of them, maybe I would have tipped. Probably I would have. But I wasn't. Besides, how would you rig mine? I fell down a flight of stairs, an empty flight of stairs with nobody around. No stair gave way, nothing like that happened at all. How am I supposed to think somebody rigged that somehow?'

He frowned. 'There's something fishy about you, Tobin,' he said. 'I'm going to check up on you, don't you worry.'

'I know you will,' I said.

He'd been sitting back in the chair, and now he leaned forward again and put his elbows on the desk top, and frowned at me as though thinking about something else. That went on for a minute or two, his expression slightly pained, as though what he was thinking about was difficult and complicated, and it took me a while to understand what it was all about.

Then I got it. He'd just finished throwing his weight around with me a little bit, and now he wanted my cooperation on something. He wanted to make the transition from cop-witness to cop-cop, and he couldn't figure out how to go about doing it.

Maybe I shouldn't have taken him off the hook, but I preferred a peaceful life to meaningless minor victories, so when at last I understood what his problem was I said, 'I know I don't have any official standing here, Captain Yoncker, and I don't want you to think I'm butting my nose into your business, but if there's anything you want me to do, any way I can be of use to you, I'll be glad to do whatever I can.'

He looked relieved, briefly, but then quickly covered that look with one of judicious consideration. 'As a matter of fact,' he said, 'you probably could help out. You've been here how long?'

'Two days,' I said. 'Since Monday.'

'Then you've had a chance to look some of these people over,' he said. 'The way I see it, I'm working at a disadvantage here, because I'm no psychiatrist, I don't know number one about nut cases, and I tell you the truth I don't trust either one of those so-called doctors. I think the both of them would try to cover up for the guilty party if they could. You know all this psychiatry stuff, it's the same as we get from the social workers all the time, they don't give a damn about the law, all they care about is how some bum is disadvantaged, that's one of the words they like. Disadvantaged. You get one of these bums, mugs somebody in an alley, you tell me which one of those two is disadvantaged. You know what I'm talking about, Tobin, you've got the same thing down in New York, only a hundred times worse.'

'I know what you're talking about,' I said. I also knew the problems he was touching on were a thousand times more complicated than either he or any of his social worker opponents would ever understand. I knew they were like the blind men trying to describe an elephant, and each describing the part he had hold of and being absolutely sure everybody else's description was dead wrong. I knew that, but I didn't know but that I was merely another blind man with another incomplete description. In any case, I was pretty sure Captain Yoncker preferred a monologue to a discussion, so I simply told him I knew what he was talking about and let it go at that.

'The way I see it,' he said, 'it could be any one of these fruitcakes. Like those two that tried to kill each other in the dining room. That kind of stuff go on all the time around here?'

'That's the first I ever heard of,' I said. 'I think the murder made everybody nervous.'

'When they start trying to kill each other like that,' he said, 'who knows what they'll do next?'

'Actually,' I said, 'those two boys didn't manage to damage one another at all. They were just wrestling. All the injury was inflicted by your men.'

He bristled a little, our relationship losing some of its cop-cop nature and teetering back toward cop-witness again. 'You sound awful damn sure of that,' he said.

'I am. I was at the next table.'

'I could have been sitting on top of those two boys,' he said, 'and I wouldn't have been able to swear who did what to who. I'd hate to have to go to court and take my oath on it, I know that much.'

'I don't see that incident ever getting to court,' I said. 'Do you?'

He looked at me. He really wasn't sure of me, and basically he didn't like what he wasn't sure of, but until he found out for sure whether I was a comrade or an opponent he was keeping his dislike in check. 'No, I don't,' he said finally. 'We took those two down to the station to cool off a while. I think by tomorrow all they're going to want is out.'

'You're probably right,' I said, and the door opened behind me.

I turned and it was the red-headed cop, the young one who'd been nervously on duty at the dining-room door. He called, in a husky whisper, as though he was trying to slide the words past me without my hearing, 'Captain? Could I see you a minute?'

Yoncker frowned at him. 'This important?'

'Yes, sir.' He was worried, but standing his ground.

Yoncker gave an exasperated sigh and heaved to his feet. 'Wait one minute, Tobin,' he said, and marched across the room and outside, closing the door behind him.

I spent this time-out in a hasty inspection of my defenses. He seemed to have accepted my story at face value, though I wouldn't rely on that entirely with a man like Yoncker. If I could keep myself small enough and quiet enough I stood a pretty good chance of getting Yoncker to think of me as a member of his team, which under the circumstances was the safest place to be. Bringing up the business about O'Hara and Merrivale had been a bad move on my part, but I hoped I'd covered it sufficiently, and I wouldn't be mentioning it again.

What would Yoncker be talking about next? From the direction he'd been leading in, I had the idea what he wanted was suggestions from me as to who the murderer might be. I already knew I wasn't going to mention my own list of suspects and non-suspects, mostly because that would reveal that I *had* known about the rigged accidents before the murder, but also partly because I disliked Yoncker intensely and had no desire to do any of his work for him.

In fact, what would I tell him when he asked me for capsule commentaries on the various residents, which he was sure to do when he came back? Edited versions of the truth, I supposed, leaving out anything he might consider social-workerish, and also leaving out anything that might prejudice him too heavily in the direction of anyone I already privately knew to be in the clear.

I was thinking about this, and working out specific answers to some of the questions I expected to be asked, when the door opened again and Yoncker came back in with a huge happy smile on his face. 'Now,' he said. 'Now, that's the way we like it.'

I turned and looked at him. 'What's happened?'

'What's happened? We've got a confession, that's what's happened.' Yoncker rubbed his hands together in pleasure. 'They can't come too easy for me,' he said. 'This is just the way I like them.'

NINETEEN

I stood in the hall doorway, Debby Lattimore's desk behind me, the door to Doctor Cameron's office beyond that, and looked down to my right, where Yoncker and his troops were with great care and great pride marching their confessed murderer this way, toward the exit.

It was Walter Stoddard. They had him in handcuffs and a uniformed cop stood on each side of him, clutching his arms above the elbow, and he walked with his head and eyes down, as though on his way to the electric chair instead of the local jail.

Stoddard? Was it merely my instinctive dislike for Yoncker that made me want to believe it hadn't really come this easy, or was there some true reason to think Stoddard was lying about himself? The faces around Stoddard were happy and self-congratulatory, hemming him in, making his face hard to see and hard to understand.

They approached me like a mini-parade, Yoncker looking directly at me to smile his wide smile, his cops all looking either straight ahead or with possessive caution at their prisoner. I kept trying to read Stoddard's down-turned face, and when they were four or five paces from me Stoddard suddenly raised his head and met my eyes, and I realized I'd had the image wrong before. It wasn't the electric chair he saw himself marching toward, it was the crucifix. The expression on his face was exactly that look of noble and self-congratulatory martyrdom that stupid painters put on the face of Christ when showing him on the way to the cross. ''Tis a far far better thing I do,' his eyes said to me, and I knew exactly what he was doing, and why. More than he did, probably.

And certainly more than Yoncker did. Yoncker passed me, and I almost spoke his name, I almost asked him to step into the privacy of the office behind me for just a minute. But then I saw myself trying to explain Walter Stoddard's mind to that man, I saw myself trying to take away his easy victory, and I knew it couldn't be done that way. Nothing I could say today would keep Yoncker from arresting Stoddard and booking him for murder.

The procession passed me by, and now I watched their

backs, and I saw that Stoddard's head was down again but his shoulders were straight, squared off. He was not morose, he was far from morose.

They went out the main entrance at last, and I heard footsteps coming the other way. I turned to look, and Doctor Fredericks was hurrying toward me down the hall. He reached me, saying, 'That was a lucky break, wasn't it? Saved a lot of agony for everybody.'

I stepped out of his way, and he came on into the office and sat at Debby Lattimore's desk to reach for the phone. 'The Brady girl is a gone goose,' he said. 'Happily she came from a place about twelve miles from here, so they can send an ambulance over and take her right back.'

'Another lucky break,' I said.

He glanced at me in surprise, holding the phone with one hand, about to dial with the other. 'What's the matter with you?'

'Make your call first,' I said.

He considered me, then shrugged and made his call. It took about five minutes, and judging from Fredericks' half of the conversation an ambulance was expected within the hour. Ringing off, Fredericks turned around to face me and said, 'Now, what is it?'

'Stoddard,' I said.

He frowned, looking past me, thinking about the man. 'I'm sorry it was him,' he said. 'In fact, I'm very surprised it was him.'

'It wasn't,' I said.

He looked at me in surprise. 'Are you sure?'

'I saw his face when they were taking him out.'

'But he confessed.'

I said, 'Stoddard's problem, the way I understand it, the problem he's been committed for in the past, is that he has overpowering feelings of guilt about having killed his daughter. He's never been able to square that account.'

Fredericks cocked his head, as if hearing an intriguing sound. 'That's possible,' he said. 'For Stoddard, yes, very possible.'

'More possible than adding more things to feel guilty about, like causing people accidents.'

'I already said he doesn't seem right for the part. Did you talk to the police about this? That Captain Yoncker?'

'No.'

'Why not?'

I shrugged. 'Would you have?'

He started to answer me, then reconsidered, thought things over, frowned, and at last shook his head. 'No, I wouldn't. But we can't very well let Stoddard take the rap like this, can we?'

'We can,' I said, 'unless we can think of something to do about it.'

'Find the right person, of course,' he said. 'That's the most obvious.'

'And the most difficult,' I pointed out. 'But the injurer might keep it up, and then we'd have a strong enough indication of Stoddard's innocence to try talking to Yoncker.'

'What if he doesn't? I mean the injurer, what if he's been scared off by all this?'

'They'll let you and Doctor Cameron talk to Stoddard, if you push hard enough,' I said. 'Try to get him to repudiate the confession.'

He said, 'What if we showed Yoncker that note you got? Stoddard doesn't know about it, and we could prove he doesn't know about it or know what it says.'

I shook my head. 'There's two things wrong with that. In the first place, once we give that note to Yoncker we let him know we knew about the rigged accidents before today. Which doesn't get Stoddard off the hook, but it puts us right back on.'

'Why doesn't it get Stoddard off the hook?'

'Because we're guessing that note came from the injurer, but we can't prove it. We won't be able to prove it to Yoncker, or a jury, or anybody. Yoncker won't give Stoddard up without a fight, and he'll bat that note right out of the park.'

'We have to turn up the real injurer,' Fredericks said, 'it's as simple as that.'

'I wish it were,' I said.

TWENTY

The day crept on. There was nothing to do, and in fact there was no real desire on anyone's part to make any kind of movement. We should have been feeling some sense of urgency, those of us who believed Stoddard's confession was a false one, but we behaved as though we'd been drugged. We were listless, without ideas and without plans and without even the nervous energy to be upset by our listlessness.

The ambulance came for Doris Brady and she was carried out on a stretcher. The residents, having felt the need to herd together so strongly at lunchtime, now obviously felt just as strong a need to be by themselves, and most took alone to their rooms.

Cameron and Fredericks and Bob Gale and I met in Cameron's office again in the late afternoon, and told one another things we all already knew. None of us managed to make any worthwhile suggestions as to what we would do next. Doctor Cameron called Captain Yoncker at Police Headquarters to find out when it would be possible to visit Stoddard, and was told it would be at least a day or two. Stoddard had phoned his wife, who would be coming to Kendrick with the family lawyer, and it would be subsequent to their arrival that Stoddard would be permitted any other visitors. Captain Yoncker also volunteered the information that a search of the local bars had not turned up Nicholas Fike, but that a man who might have been Fike had been seen at the Greyhound terminal. No one knew what bus he had taken, if any.

That made us discuss, in a desultory way, the possibility that the injurer really was Nicholas Fike after all, but none of us could see it that way. His history showed no links with that kind of anti-social activity, and as Fredericks pointed out, it was next to impossible that Fike could have done any of that trap-laying without settling his nerves with alcohol.

What about Doris Brady? We rolled that idea around a while, trying to find some way to believe it. We suggested that she had been the injurer, and that she had gone into shock as a result of one of her booby traps resulting in death rather than merely injury. For motive we tried to build a case out of her desire to do to others on a physical level what had been done to her on a psychic level, the sudden pulling out of the rug from under all her values and assumptions. We made a case that was neither persuasive nor totally ludicrous, and were left at the end with a possibility, though remote. And as Bob Gale said, if Doris Brady really was the injurer, it would be very tough to prove, since Doris was totally unavailable for questioning.

Who else was there? O'Hara and Merrivale, both now cooling their heels at the local jail, still had to be considered active suspects. Either one of them, feeling the panic of guilt, might have precipitated that fight in the dining room. The only thing wrong was, the fight only implied panic, not necessarily guilt.

Which left only six people from the suspect list still present in The Midway, and five of them were women, the lone man being Jerry Kanter. The women were Debby Lattimore, Ethel Hall, Helen Dorsey, Ruth Enhrengart and Ivy Pollett. I myself found it impossible to believe it was Debby, and almost impossible to believe it was Ruth Ehrengart, the woman who'd had a nervous breakdown after the birth of her tenth child. Ethel Hall, the lesbian librarian, I also considered virtually guaranteed to be innocent. Helen Dorsey, the compulsive housekeeper, and Ivy Pollett, the victim of plots and stratagems and myriad attempted rapes, seemed to me a little more likely, but not very. Which left Jerry Kanter, whom I disliked for unworthy reasons and who was in an odd way too blithely healthy to be the guilty party.

Which brought us back to those suspects no longer in the house: O'Hara and Merrivale, Doris Brady and Nicholas Fike.

It was getting us nowhere going over and over that list of ten names. We could give opinions and prejudices, we could invent theories and potential motivations, but we couldn't with one hundred per cent assurance cross out any one of those ten names. Nor could any of us think of anything constructive to do. Our conference ended at dinnertime with nothing having been accomplished and no plans having been made to accomplish anything at any later date.

Bob and I had a mostly silent dinner together in a mostly empty dining room. Only a few hardy souls, like Edgar Jennings and Helen Dorsey and George Bartholomew, sat spaced around at the various tables, and most of them ate quickly and alone and soon left to return to their rooms.

We saw a number of people come down and go directly through to the kitchen and return with trays or paper bags, planning to eat in the solitude and safety of their rooms, and these moved by us without meeting anyone's eye. Ivy Pollett was one of them, and Donald Walburn, and Rose Ackerson. Rose came through three times while we ate, carrying the same tray back and forth every time, and after the third trip Bob said, 'Suppose she's bringing food to everybody upstairs?'

'Just to Molly Schweitzler,' I said. 'I think I ought to mention that to Doctor Cameron. Those two are both going directly back into their sick behavior patterns.'

But everybody was, really. Ivy Pollett had come through with a hunted look on her face, the paranoid unable to trust anyone, beginning to suspect the plots and schemes again. Across the way, Helen Dorsey was behaving in small odd ways alone at her table, organizing dishes and silverware, scrubbing everything with her napkin, treating her food as something excremental that had to be removed from what she meant to be a department store place-setting. The entire population of The Midway could be felt slipping backward into the safety of compulsive behavior. The murder had started it, the presence and manner of the police had intensified it, and now it seemed to be rolling along on its own momentum. Finding the true killer might save Stoddard — who, of course, had also fallen backwards into his particular kind of compulsion — but would it make any difference to these crumbling personalities all around me? It might be like bringing the antibiotic after the epidemic has already swept through.

But the question was academic, since at the moment we had no antibiotic and no idea how to get hold of it, and the epidemic was running its course unchecked.

After dinner I met with Doctor Cameron again, to tell him some of the problem behavior I'd been noticing, particularly Rose Ackerson and Molly Schweitzler, but he already knew about most of it and felt just as powerless as I did. 'We'll have to let them shake this out for a while,' he said. 'And hope when it's all over we'll be able to repair the damage.'

He had a fairly extensive library of books on psychiatry in a small room off his office, and I borrowed several that looked from the titles as though they might be useful. I took them up to my room and spent the evening dipping into book after book, following chapter titles and then footnotes and ultimately wild guesses. I found several things disturbing to me personally, which I hurried past the way we hurry past vomit on the sidewalk, but there was nothing in particular to help me in my job of winnowing ten names down to one, and at last I went to bed and had confused and mournful dreams and awoke at seven-thirty in the morning with a vague but simple idea in my head.

TWENTY-ONE

The four of us sat around in Doctor Cameron's office, and the general atmosphere was really not much different from yesterday. It was nine-thirty in the morning now and sunlight poured in through the windows behind the desk, making the room brighter than it had been yesterday afternoon. But the three faces around me looked just as dim and lethargic, and I found their listlessness bringing back my own, so that instead of suggesting my idea at once, I held it back. I listened to the others chew the same old sentences over again while I picked my idea to pieces and started finding things wrong with it. You can always find things wrong with every idea, if you really want to.

But that was foolish, and in one of the lulls in the conversation – the conversation being half lulls – I finally forced myself to say, 'I have an idea.' Though I couldn't let it go at that, but had to add, 'A small idea, I don't know if it will do any good.'

Any idea was a sign of life, of course, and they all looked at me with interest. Fredericks said, 'It has to do more good than our just sitting around here moaning at one another.'

I said, 'What I was thinking was that we do have some physical hints about the injurer. Not what he looks like, but things he's used. Like a saw, for instance. And the paper when he wrote me that note. And he had at least one little bottle of Scotch. It seems to me if I could search the rooms of the people on my suspect list there just might be something useful to be found. Not even real proof necessarily, just an indication of who we should lean on.'

Doctor Cameron said, 'But if he knows you're searching, he'll get rid of anything that might incriminate him.'

I said, 'That's why I thought it might be a good idea to make this morning's group therapy session compulsory. In fact, both sessions today could be compulsory. The way people are breaking down it would be a good idea anyway, but we could arrange our lists so all the suspects are in the morning session. There's only six of them still in the house.'

Everybody thought that was a fine idea. At least, everybody

thought it was an idea, and it gave us something to do, something to think about, and that was fine.

We immediately made up our two lists for the two compulsory group therapy sessions, putting the six suspects – Jerry Kanter, Debby Lattimore, Ethel Hall, Helen Dorsey, Ruth Ehrengart and Ivy Pollett – in the morning session with Edgar Jennings and Phil Roche, two of the cleared ping-pong players. There were only fifteen people in the house now, out of the original twenty-two, so that left seven for the afternoon session.

The session would be at ten-thirty, so Bob left at once with the list to let all the residents know about it, and Fredericks and Cameron and I sat around the office a while longer, talking about what would happen if we didn't manage to come up with a replacement for Stoddard. Captain Yoncker had taken the names and home addresses of all the residents, and at least some of them would eventually be called upon to testify, at least at the coroner's inquest if not at the actual murder trial. We three could be sure of having to testify at both. There hadn't been any activity from the news media yet, mostly because Kendrick was serviced only by a weekly newspaper that considered its job adequately completed if it kept on top of the church socials. But there had to be at least one local wire-service stringer and we could expect reporters to start sniffing around sooner or later. Murder in a loony bin.

At a quarter after ten Doctor Cameron went away to take charge of the morning group therapy session and I went upstairs to my room to wait till the coast was clear. Bob Gale came up about fifteen minutes later and said, 'The morning session's in there now.'

I'd been lying on the bed, resting and thinking about my arm, which had started itching madly today under the cast. I sat up and tried to ease the itching by turning my wrist back and forth, but there was hardly any leeway inside the cast and when I forced it I got a sharp pain up my arm to my shoulder for my troubles. I said, 'Shouldn't I be seeing a doctor about this thing?'

Bob said, 'Your arm? I heard him tell Doctor Cameron after he put the cast on that you should go to see him over at the hospital next Monday.'

'Next Monday,' I repeated. Would I still be here next Monday? Today was Thursday, my fourth day at The Midway, next Monday would be the start of my second week here. Would I really be here that long? And if so, what good would I have done by then? All I'd done so far was root out a harmless little stowaway and hound him to his death. Not an accomplishment I felt particularly proud of.

Bob said, 'We ought to start, Mr. Tobin. They'll only be in there for an hour.'

'You're right,' I said, and got to my feet. 'Let's go.'

'Who do you want to start with?'

'Jerry Kanter.'

Bob led me to Jerry's room, and stood guard outside while I went on in. There were no locks on any of the doors at The Midway, a lack for which there was some sort of psychological theory I never understood, mostly because I never particularly cared.

The rooms in The Midway were all different, and yet all the same. The shapes were different, each to each, partly because that had been the original plan of the house and partly as a result of the renovations the place had suffered over the years. But the furnishings were essentially the same, and when we look at a room we tend first to look at the furniture in it and only later, if ever, do we look at the shape and design and impression of the room itself.

Jerry Kanter's room, therefore, at first reminded me strongly of my own room, and Doris Brady's room, and Nicholas Fike's room; but this time I was interested in the differences, not the similarities. It was smaller than mine, and had only the one window, which overlooked the roof of the nineteenth-century carport outside the main entrance at the side of the house. There was a *Playboy* centerfold over the bed, which in the surroundings I found bizarre and somehow disturbing. The bed was neatly made, in a way that made me think of Army barracks. The closet, when I opened it, was also neat, every shirt and coat and jacket lined up and facing the same way, leftward, which would most likely make Kanter right-handed.

There was a small framed picture on the metal bureau, which when I looked at it closely turned out to be a shot of Kapp's Kar Wash, showing three cars on line in front of the entrance. There were no human beings visible in the picture.

The bottom drawer of the bureau contained several paperback books. *The 1969 Buying Guide Issue of Consumer Reports. All About Tipping. Practical Business Mathematics. Goldfinger. Thunderball. Six Weeks to Words of Power. Man Hungry. Passion Doll. The Power of Positive Thinking.*

There was nothing hidden behind or under any bureau drawer. Nothing hidden anywhere in the closet or behind any furniture or anywhere in the bed. I could find no loose floorboards, no wall panels, no break in the ceiling. There was nothing else to remark on in the room.

I went out and Bob gave me a questioning look and I shook my head. He shrugged and said, 'Who next?'

'It doesn't matter. Anybody that's handy, among those in the session downstairs. People like O'Hara and Merrivale, who aren't in the building at all, we can let go till later.'

'Ethel Hall's room is right across the hall here.'

So I did that one next, and it too reminded me of my own room, but most forcibly reminded me of it as it was when I'd first walked into it. Ethel Hall had made practically no impression at all on this place. I had to open the closet door and the bureau drawers to find anything actually owned by her. She had no pictures, no books, virtually no possessions other than clothing, except that in the bottom drawer of the bureau were seven pairs of glasses, neatly packed away under a gray cardigan sweater. She wore glasses, rectangle wire-frame, and these seven pairs were all exactly the same style. I looked through them, and they all seemed to be the same prescription, though I couldn't be absolutely sure about that. They didn't seem to be all that strong, though, and I was surprised at the force of her fear of being without eye-glasses, that would lead her to have seven spares.

This room too was empty of hiding places that I could find, and Bob led me next to Debby Lattimore's room, which was reminiscent of nothing but Debby. She had added curtains of her own to the room's two windows, had put her own pink and white bedspread on the bed, and her bureau top was crowded with small and large photos in various kinds of frames. About half were of boys her age, some in uniform but most not, and the rest were apparently family members. All were smiling, and some had small statements or signatures written on the lower right corners. The whole room had a faint scent which I recognized immediately as Debby's even though I'd never consciously noticed before that Debby wore any scent.

A bureau drawer produced two stacks of letters held by loose red rubber bands. The first was from her mother, and the general tone throughout all the letters, which had apparently been written almost daily since she'd arrived here at The Midway, was a terrible nervousness ineffectively trying to conceal itself behind chatter. The letters frequently mentioned the enclosure of a check, and far too frequently reassured Debby that Dad was anxiously and eagerly waiting for her to come home. 'Everything will be fine now.' That sentence rang again and again and again, until it came to mean exactly the opposite of what the words said. I imagined Debby was a smart enough girl to see that for herself.

The other stack of letters was from a boy who loved her but who was afraid to involve himself with someone who'd been committed to an asylum. He couldn't bring himself to give her up altogether, and yet he couldn't take the chance and commit himself all the way. His letters were far less frequent than the letters from 'Mother', as she signed herself, but his were much longer. He didn't try to hide the ambivalence of his feelings, but tortured himself – and her, I was sure – by endless monologues on the subject, trying to talk himself around to one conclusion or the other. His references to her letters led me to believe that she for her part was involved in the same sort of self-torture, not sure whether to renounce the boy or take the chance of guaranteeing her future self to him. The most recent letters in both stacks were very nearly carbon copies of the oldest, nothing having progressed or changed in either place.

Ruth Ehrengart's room was next, and here one entire wall was full of snapshots. thumbtacked to the wall in endless monotonous rows. The ten children, over and over, singly and in every possible combination. Smiling, crying, frowning, playing, fighting. Squinting in sunlight in the summer, gloating under a Christmas tree in the winter. Was Ruth Ehrengart trying to become familiar with her devil in hopes of overcoming it that way? Then why were there so few photos of the man who must be her husband, a large and burly man, always smiling, frequently in his undershirt, most often sitting down. He looked like an honest, amiable workman, about whom the sea of children eddied and flowed unnoticed.

Debby had had much more than the usual amount of clothing, overflowing both closet and bureau, and now Ruth Ehrengart restored the balance by having much less. And the clothing she did have was mostly drab. New-looking for the most part, but with a cheap washed-out quality they must already have possessed when she'd picked them out in the store. I poked through this meager supply, and found nothing.

Helen Dorsey's room matched Helen Dorsey's character to a T. It was spotless, but it went beyond spotlessness to actual discomfort. The two windows weren't merely clean, they had a sort of sparkling film over them that made them glint painfully in my eyes as I walked around the room. The air had a distasteful stink of ammonia to it, and when I touched the metal bureau it made a squeaking sound that rippled my backbone.

Her bed and closet were military perfection, even more so than Jerry Kanter's, and in the back of the closet were mop, broom, bucket, basket of cleaning cloths, various cans and bottles of soaps and cleansers, all lined up for inspection. The closet smelled strongly of them all.

I searched Helen Dorsey's room as thoroughly as the others, but it too had nothing of actual incrimination to offer. In police parlance, it was clean.

Ivy Pollett had a radio hidden in a bureau drawer. Not a ham outfit, a sending set, nothing like that. An ordinary AM radio, a small compact model hidden under a folded skirt. I took it out and plugged it in, without changing the setting of the dial, and a local station came on, playing Paul Weston music. It had been quite a while since I'd heard Paul Weston music. I left the radio on while I searched the room, finding nothing but that Ivy Pollett was secretly sloppy – dirty clothes made a mound on the floor just inside the closet door – and when the Paul Weston music ended an announcer came on to remind us that this station offered news every half-hour, twenty-four hours a day. Then Hugo Winterhalter music started, and I unplugged the radio again and put it back where I'd found it. There was nothing else of interest in the room.

I came back out to the hall again, and once more shook my head, and Bob said, 'That's all of them.'

'The six downstairs in the group therapy session.'

'Right.'

'We have four others,' I said. 'Fike. He took off with a suitcase, so I doubt there's any point checking his room. Doris Brady. Doctor Cameron can do that one himself later on, without anybody wondering why.'

Marilyn Nazarro and Beth Tracy came walking down the hall, and Bob and I talked about ping-pong until they'd gone by and out of sight around the next corner. There were still half a dozen residents wandering around at the moment, which was why Bob had been standing guard in front of each door as I'd worked.

When we were alone again, Bob said, 'That leaves O'Hara and Merrivale.'

I looked at my watch, and it was eleven twenty-five. The group therapy session would last another five minutes. 'Let's get to them,' I said.

It was easy shorthand to think of O'Hara and Merrivale together, partly because they looked so much alike and partly because they almost always *were* together, but once inside their rooms the differences glared. Merrivale, the father-beater, had a room so laden with working-man-masculine symbols you could almost smell the sweat. Two photos on the bureau showed Merrivale respectively in a black leather jacket while sitting astride a Harley-Davidson motorcycle, one of the big ones, and the other wearing hunting clothes, rifle in hands, foot on the neck of a dead deer in a forest setting. Copies of *Playboy* and its imitators formed one stack on the closet floor, and copies of the gamier imitators of *True* formed another. Half a dozen paperback sex novels, similar to the two I'd found in Jerry Kanter's bureau, were stacked on the closet shelf, beside a visored cap of the sort worn by military men and bus drivers. The clothing all tended toward the tough, and under the mattress of his unmade bed I found two long one-by-twelve planks, apparently put in there to keep William Merrivale from succumbing to the lewd luxury of a too-soft mattress. Seeing all this, I was amazed he'd contented himself with mouthing off at me after I'd hit Fredericks, instead of immediately lunging at me with ringing cries.

Robert O'Hara's room possibly showed an earlier stage of the same road, but possibly not. There was no way to be sure. He had baseball cards in his bureau drawer, comic books on the closet shelf, and he'd built himself a simple bookcase out of pine boards, in which there was nothing but boy's books. *Tom Swift, Junior. Christopher Cool, Teen Agent. Dave Dawson. The Boy Allies.*

But what childhood did he want? The Boy Allies were from the First World War, long before both his time and mine. *The Boy Allies at Jutland* was one of the titles he had, and did he even know the significance of the place Jutland? I myself vaguely remembered there'd been some sort of Naval battle there in World War One, but that was all.

Dave Dawson was my childhood, not his. World War Two, Dave Dawson and his English friend, Freddy Farmer. I had those books myself at one time, but they were long gone. *Dave*

Dawson at Libya, he had. *Dave Dawson on the Russian Front*. I remembered those titles, remembered the pictures on the bedraggled dust jackets. I stood there holding *Dave Dawson on the Russian Front* and found myself remembering my room when I was a boy. The rug on the floor, the small bookcase in which I kept not only Dave Dawson, but also The Lone Ranger, Tom Swift (outdated already then, but not yet overtaken by Junior) and half a dozen others. Books about Indians, frequently the Iroquois. Books about Robin Hood and various knights, their opponents usually Black, but not in any modern sense. I stood there quite a long time, remembering, thinking back to a time when just about all my mistakes were still in front of me, and I found myself getting angry at Robert O'Hara, as though in some obscure way he was stealing my childhood from me.

But where was his childhood? Tom Swift, Junior, and Christopher Cool, Teen Agent, were both too recent. That was my suspicion, and a look at the copyright dates inside the books confirmed it. It was every childhood but his own that Robert O'Hara, the incorrigible child-molester, was trying to amass. Why?

Of all the rooms, this one held me the longest. I felt a confusion about this boy, a melancholy that linked some sort of chain between us. I couldn't understand why, and I wanted to.

A knock at the door roused me at last. I went over and opened it, and Bob said urgently, 'You better hurry, Mr. Tobin. I hear them coming upstairs.'

'I'm done,' I said, leaving O'Hara's room at once because I didn't want to leave it at all.

'Wasn't there anything there either?'

I shook my head. We'd done all the rooms, my idea had worked itself out, nothing had come of it. I felt very discouraged, and very tired. 'I'm going to my room,' I said. 'Would you tell Doctor Cameron I didn't find anything, and I'll be down to talk to him later.'

'Sure.' He looked at me, worried about me, and I knew he was trying to think of something encouraging to say, but of course there was nothing. And then people began arriving on the second floor, and there was nothing more to say at all. He turned one way and I the other.

The group was behind me, individuals dropping off at their own rooms. I reached mine, and went inside, and a small handsaw was lying on the bed.

A handsaw? I shut the door and went over to it, and a piece of notepaper was lying on it, the same sort of notepaper as the first time. And written on in the same way, all capital letters, ballpoint pen. Saying:

WALTER STODDARD DIDN'T DO
IT. I DID IT. WITH THIS.

TWENTY-TWO

Doctor Cameron read the note and then handed it across the desk to Doctor Fredericks, who frowned at it quickly and then said to me, 'Where's the saw?'

'In my closet,' I said. 'I doubt there's any prints on it, everybody in the world knows about fingerprints by now, but just to be on the safe side I handled it carefully, wrapped it in an undershirt and put it on the shelf in my closet.'

It was just the three of us in Cameron's office now, Bob Gale not having been here when I'd walked in, though he'd been by to deliver my discouraging message. Now, of course, things were different.

Doctor Cameron said, 'I don't understand why the note. Why the saw. Why any of it.'

'Our injurer is feeling guilty at last,' I said. 'He doesn't want somebody else punished for his crime. He passed the word on to me because he had the idea, from the incident in the dining room probably, that I was some sort of liaison to the local police.'

'But why give you the saw?'

'Proof of some sort, I suppose. Maybe he thought there'd be some way to match it to the cuts he made. Or it could be demonstrated that Walter Stoddard couldn't describe the saw that did the cutting.'

Fredericks said, 'I think mainly it was a symbol. Not only symbolic proof that the note really was from the injurer, but also proof that he doesn't intend to do any more of it. He's sorry, and he's quitting.'

Doctor Cameron said, 'Do we take this note and saw to Captain Yoncker?'

'Of course,' Fredericks said.

I said, 'No.' They both looked at me, about to argue, and I said, 'This isn't any more proof than the first note was. And neither is the saw. Any saw could have been used, not necessarily that one. Captain Yoncker isn't going to give up a confessed murderer without a struggle. If we bring him that note and the saw, we're liable to get put behind bars ourselves for manufacturing evidence.'

Fredericks said, angrily, 'Damn it, man, why is nothing ever good enough? Why is nothing ever a reason to take action?'

'We have a reason to take action,' I said. 'But the right action, not the wrong action.'

'What's the right action?'

'You haven't noticed something,' I said, and when Fredericks looked down at the note he was still holding I said, 'Not in the wording of the note. In the timing of its delivery.'

He frowned at me, suspecting irrelevance. 'What do you mean, the timing? It came after the murder, naturally.'

'It came,' I told him, 'while Doctor Cameron was in the group therapy session with our entire list of present suspects.' I turned to Cameron, saying, 'Did anybody leave the room at any time for any reason during the hour?'

'No one,' he said.

Fredericks said, 'What are you suggesting? That Fike is hanging around, he's slipped back into the building and left that note?'

'No, and I'm not suggesting that O'Hara or Merrivale slipped out of jail either, or that Doris Brady is faking her catatonia.'

Fredericks spread his hands. 'That's your entire suspect list,' he said.

'I know it. It means we made a mistake somewhere very early on. It means the injurer never was on the suspect list at all. Because the only person who could have left that note and the saw was one of the seven residents not in this morning's session. Because the session had already started when I left my room and was just over when I got back to my room, meaning nobody in the session would have had the opportunity to do it.'

Doctor Cameron said, 'But we've already eliminated everyone else.'

'We were wrong,' I said. 'We cleared somebody we shouldn't have cleared.'

Fredericks made a disgusted sound and said, 'That's fine. Three days later we find out we're working with the wrong list.'

'It happens,' I said. I saw no point wasting time trying to defend myself in Fredericks' eyes.

Doctor Cameron said, 'Well, who are the people now? Seven, you say?'

'Six, really,' I told him, 'since Bob Gale was with me the whole time. We were never close enough to my room for him to have dashed away to a hiding place, gotten the note and

138

saw, ducked them into my room and got back to me without my coming out of whatever room I was searching and finding him gone.'

Doctor Cameron pulled notepaper and pencil toward himself and said, 'Who are the six?'

'Marilyn Nazarro. Beth Tracy. Rose Ackerson. Molly Schweitzler. Donald Walburn. And George Bartholomew.'

He wrote the names down as I said them and then studied them, frowning. 'Four of these we can eliminate right away,' he said. 'They're among the injured. That would only leave Marilyn Nazarro and Beth Tracy.' He looked at me. 'Why did we assume they were cleared?'

'They were among the group in the ping-pong room when the staircase was rigged, the time I got this arm.'

Fredericks said, 'There were half a dozen people in that room. Bob said nobody left, but how could he be that sure? He was involved in the games, not counting heads.'

Doctor Cameron said, 'So it's one of these two girls. Marilyn Nazarro or Beth Tracy.'

'Not necessarily,' I said. 'It could still be one of the other four.'

'But they were all victims.' He studied the list on his desk. 'Weren't they? Yes. Rose and Molly with the table in the dining room, George Bartholomew with the bed frame in the closet, Donald Walburn with the ladder.' He looked up at me. 'You aren't suggesting one of these people injured *himself*, are you? On purpose?'

'Possibly,' I said.

Fredericks said, 'To divert attention from himself, you mean.'

'That's one reason. It isn't the only possible reason. Look, we've been assuming all along that the motive for all this is an irrational one, and we can't leave out the possibility that the injurer felt he himself should be one of the victims.'

'That's possible,' Fredericks said doubtfully. 'It isn't probable.'

'Nothing that's taken place here is probable,' I told him. 'I wouldn't have expected the probable here. But it is possible. And it's possible that one of those accidents wasn't rigged at all, that it's a simple matter of biter bit.'

'We know the ladder was,' Doctor Cameron said. 'I saw the sawn-through rung myself.'

'That leaves Walburn out to that extent,' I said. 'But what

139

about the others? George Bartholomew could be the injurer, and being hit with the bed frame was pure accident – and he could have been poking around in that closet for something to use in one of his booby traps. Or that table that collapsed in the dining room simply collapsed, without being rigged at all.'

'You're becoming more and more improbable,' Fredericks told me.

I said, 'I don't want to make the same mistake twice. Physical laws of possibility have narrowed the list down to these six people. No one else could have put the note and the saw in my room. I don't want to cut any of them at all off the list on the basis of guesses and suppositions, because all I have are the same guesses and suppositions that made me make the mistake in the first place. This time I'm sure I have the injurer on my list, and I don't want to take the chance of letting him slip off it again.'

Fredericks said, 'All right, I see the point. So what do you want to do? Search rooms again?'

'As a matter of fact,' I said, 'yes. But this time it's simpler, I'm simply looking for paper to match the two notes I was sent. I should be able to go through the six rooms in a quarter of an hour. Whether I find the paper or not, I'll come down to the therapy session when I'm done. We'll know we have the injurer somewhere at that table with us. With or without the paper, we'll do what we can.'

'Do what we can? Meaning what?'

'Meaning,' I said, 'it will be a lot simpler to deal with Yoncker if we can hand him another confession.'

The dining room was almost empty when I went into it for lunch. Only one table was occupied, by George Bartholomew and Donald Walburn. I went over and said, 'Mind if I join you?'

It was Bartholomew who looked up, showing me again the healing but still angry scars on his cheek and around his mouth. Deliberately self-inflicted? It was hard to believe. 'Well, sure,' he said. 'Sit down.'

Donald Walburn didn't say anything at all, and didn't even look up from his plate. He was eating noodle soup, slowly, steadily, mechanically, but a kind of hyper-awareness flowed out from him. He was braced against my presence, and I could feel it like a physical wall between us.

This was the closest I'd been to Walburn, though I'd seen him a few times before, moving slowly along on the crutches now leaning against the wall behind him. A slight, hawk-nosed man in his late forties, Donald Walburn had spent most of his latter teens and twenties in various prisons on various charges of burglary or petty larceny, but since his last prison term ended sixteen years ago he'd apparently trod the straight and narrow. He had never married, and lived off-and-on with a married brother and his family. He did factory work, mostly, occasionally drove a cab, and the trouble apparently started about six years ago when he got into an argument with a foreman on one job he held, who used his old prison record to have him fired. He began to mistrust everybody after that, to believe that the foreman was following him from job to job, trying to make trouble for him. Eventually, he came to the conclusion that the foreman was simply the agent for a group of toughs who had dominated one of the prisons he'd been in fifteen years before, and he believed that this group had decided for the fun of it to harass and prey upon him the rest of his life. He blamed the group for his never having married, for the increasing bitterness that was growing between himself and his brother's family, for the increasing trouble he was having holding down a job, for everything that was going wrong and had gone wrong in his entire life. He ultimately attacked a perfect stranger in a bar, slashing him with a broken bottle, because he thought him to be one of the group;

his manner after his arrest led to a psychiatric examination and finally to a commitment of four years in a state mental hospital. His dossier did not claim he was cured, but only that he had learned to deal with and control his problems, which meant he still harbored the same suspicions about the prison group but would probably no longer take any overt action against them. It was very likely he blamed the group for the ladder rung that gave way beneath him, breaking his leg, and looking at him across the table now I found it very difficult to believe he had done it to himself.

Though not impossible. It seemed as though nothing was impossible in The Midway. And the dossier on Donald Walburn could be inaccurate in its prognosis. Walburn might simply have learned to make his counterattacks more subtle than an attack with a broken bottle. Rigged accidents, perhaps.

The waitress today was Debby Lattimore, who brought my soup and gave me a tense smile, then took away Walburn's and Bartholomew's empty soup plates and went back to the kitchen. I started to eat, and George Bartholomew said, 'I didn't think you'd still be here.'

I looked at him. 'Why not?'

'Everything's cleared up, isn't it?' He was the nervous fortyish kleptomaniac and string-saver who had been released from the institution not because he was cured but because he was harmless. But was he? He said, 'You've found that fellow who was hiding, and Walter admitted causing all these accidents,' his hand strayed to his injured face, 'so I thought you'd be leaving now.'

Donald Walburn threw me a quick hard glance and looked back down at his empty place. Debby was coming back, bringing two plates of that kind of outsize hamburger usually called Salisbury steak and frequently served in places where large numbers of people are being fed without a choice of menu.

I said, 'I will be leaving in a day or two, I suppose. But I've had some personal problems I wanted to talk over with Doctor Cameron and Doctor Fredericks. I haven't had much time up till now.'

He nodded, satisfied. Debby put down the two plates, and that ended conversation for a while. I went on eating my soup.

Rose Ackerson entered the room, carrying an empty tray. Looking at no one, she walked the length of the room and went into the kitchen. A minute later Helen Dorsey and Ruth

Ehrengart came in and took a table across the room from us. Debby came out with soup for them, by which time I was finished with mine and she came over to take the plate away. As she went into the kitchen, Rose Ackerson came out again, the tray now piled high with food, tending heavily to sugars and starches. She ignored everyone again on her way through the room.

Salisbury steak is another main course that can be cut with a fork, which saved me the embarrassment of asking Bartholomew to cut up my food for me. I was getting more used to working left-handed now, and I ate at a good pace.

Marilyn Nazarro and Beth Tracy came in and sat at another table, and I glanced over at them but didn't stare. They were now both suddenly on the revised suspect list, and I was going to have to give them more attention than I had up till now.

Marilyn Nazarro was the twenty-seven-year-old woman who'd married while still in high school, had twins and another child in the first three years of marriage, and gradually developed severe symptoms of a manic-depressive cycle. She'd been in mental hospitals twice, for two years and then for three years, and though she seemed cheerful and normal enough now, the prognosis was poor, primarily because no matter what was done for her in the hospital, every time she came out she had no choice but to return to the same life as before.

Beth Tracy, a pretty if vague-looking blonde of twenty-three, was simply a sex-hysteric. Her marriage had been annulled by her husband for non-consummation, she'd tried three times to kill herself, and she was frank that the whole idea of sexual intercourse was the most disgusting and terrifying thing she could think of. The doctors believed the problem was rooted in some incident in the past, but had been unable to find it. Beth Tracy was another ex-patient released not because she was cured but because she had learned to some extent to live with her insufficiencies. She knew better now than to establish any romantic liaison with anybody.

Was either of these the injurer? Manic-depressives and sex-hysterics tend to hurt no one but themselves, at least not physically, whatever the psychological damage they may do to the people around them.

But what about the two right here at my table? A kleptomaniac and a man with a persecution complex. George Bartholomew, the kleptomaniac, had always been as harmless as

143

a rabbit and it was hard to see him any other way. Donald Walburn, the persecuted, had been violent in the past, but openly so and with a specific target. The scattergun effect of the injurer's booby traps made it hard to fit any motive at all, including a Donald Walburn's misguided attempts to get even with a nonexistent conspiracy.

My other two possibles were not in the room, and wouldn't be. Rose Ackerson was obviously feeding both herself and Molly Schweitzler with those trays of food she kept coming down for. The one a lonely woman who had kidnapped a child in an attempt to have a child of her own again, the other a lonely woman who had reacted to real or imagined rejections by compulsive overeating. They had found one another, they obviously filled needs for one another, but from the amount of food going upstairs I thought they were filling those needs in an unhealthy way. Rose and Molly had not merely become mother and child, they had become indulgent mother and spoiled child, which wasn't good for either of them.

But where in their self-contained universe would there be a need for causing pain and accidents to other people? Why would either of them have caused an accident to both the other one and to herself?

I didn't like my list of six suspects, not at all. But it was the only list I had.

There was ice cream for dessert. Donald Walburn had rushed through his meal and gone, but George Bartholomew had taken his time, so that he and I started our dessert simultaneously. I saw him glancing at me out of the corner of his eye, and understood he had another question he wanted to ask me. There was nothing to do but brace myself and wait till he was ready.

He wasn't ready till his ice cream was all finished and he'd started on his coffee. Then he said, 'I've been thinking.'

I looked at him. 'Oh?'

He met my look, his eyes level but troubled. 'About Walter,' he said. 'Do you suppose there's any chance he didn't do it?'

I weighed my answer, and finally said, 'I don't know. That would be up to the police to decide.'

He nodded somberly. 'I suppose so,' he said. 'It just doesn't seem like Walter, if you know what I mean.'

'I know what you mean,' I said, and left it there, and went upstairs to rest up for the afternoon.

TWENTY-FOUR

The session had been going on for twenty minutes when I walked in, and everyone was there who was supposed to be there. Donald Walburn was talking as I entered, and he promptly clapped his mouth shut and turned to give me a suspicious glare.

'I'm sorry I'm late,' I said, ostensibly to Doctor Fredericks.

'That's all right, Tobin,' he said. 'Sit down.'

'Thank you,' I said, and as I sat down I met Fredericks' eye again and shook my head slightly. I had not found the matching notepaper. My search, necessarily fast and superficial, had not turned up anything useful.

Fredericks pursed his lips slightly in irritation, then let the expression fade as he turned to Walburn. 'Nobody's questioning the fact that the ladder was cut, Donald,' he said, 'no more than anybody's questioning the fact that Frank DeWitt is dead. But the person who arranged all these accidents wasn't trying to hurt *you* in particular any more than he was trying to kill Frank DeWitt. Don't you see that?'

'All I see,' Walburn said, his voice harsh and low, as though he was unused to using it, 'is that I got a broken leg, and somebody did it on purpose. How do I know *all* them things weren't aimed at hurting me?'

Marilyn Nazarro, across the table from me, said, 'Why, Mr. Walburn, that's just the sort of thing you said you weren't going to believe any more.'

'Well, maybe I was just right to begin with,' Walburn told her.

'We've gone through this before, Donald,' Fredericks said, and proceeded to go through it again. While he did, I looked around at the others sitting at the long oval table in the group therapy room. I was midway along the right side, with Beth Tracy to my right and Doctor Fredericks past her at the head of the table. To my left was George Bartholomew, and then an empty chair, and then Donald Walburn, sitting apart from the rest of us but not quite all the way around to the foot of the table.

Across the way, Bob Gale sat on Fredericks' other side. Bob wasn't a suspect, but in order not to raise any questions in the others' minds he had to be present, since he'd been scheduled all along for the afternoon session.

To Bob's right sat Marilyn Nazarro, looking at Donald Walburn with friendly concern. Past her was an empty space, not quite wide enough for someone else to sit there, and then Rose Ackerson, watching each speaker in turn with a guarded expression on her face. Beyond Rose, and in a sense hidden by her, shielded by her, was Molly Schweitzler, and when I got my first look at her I blinked in astonishment. Was it possible for a person to noticeably gain weight overnight? Or was that apparent new heaviness simply a new laxity in the way Molly held her head and her body? She *looked* fatter, and as I watched her her hand came up from her lap and put some- thing in her mouth. She was looking at no one in particular, she seemed absorbed in idle daydreamy interior thoughts of her own, and she slowly chewed and swallowed what she'd put in her mouth. Then her hand came up again, and fed her some more.

What did she have in her lap? A bag of candy, maybe, or a piece of cake. Something that she could just keep nibbling at throughout the session, the taste in her mouth distracting her from all outside pressures, from all thought.

Sometimes there's a fascination in repugnant things, and that was true at that moment of Molly Schweitzler. I watched her until I felt Rose Ackerson glaring at me, and then I re- luctantly turned my eyes and my attention away and tried to concentrate on what I was here for.

Walburn was still talking, arguing with whomever would answer back. His point remained the same; that the accident that had broken his leg had been specifically aimed at him, and that all the others had probably been aimed at him. He spoke with a gloomy sort of satisfaction, as though having finally learned to live with the worst, he thought he could maybe go on from here. I looked past George Bartholomew at Walburn's pinched face, and I found it impossible to believe he was acting. He really did suspect himself to be the intended victim of a scattergun plot with who knew how many plotters. And if that were true, how could he have been the one to set the traps?

In any case, I wanted to hear from some of the others, not exclusively from Walburn, so the next time there was a pause in his low-pitched polemic I said, 'I don't know about all that. I got caught too, you know. I got this arm out of it. But I don't believe the weakened fire escape was aimed at Dewey. I don't believe any of it was aimed at anybody. You never made a habit of going out on that fire escape, did you?' I didn't want an answer to that, and rushed on, covering the couple of words he started to say in response. 'The same with what happened to Bartholomew here,' I said. 'In the first place, you wouldn't have been the one to go down and open that closet door, he would. And in the second place, I bet *he* doesn't think this whole thing was aimed at *him*.' I looked at Bartholomew. 'Do you?'

'I think it was just to hurt everybody,' Bartholomew said. 'Not even to kill anybody, not that fellow Dewey or DeWitt or whatever his name was, not anybody. Just to hurt people. And whoever did it, I don't think he cared *who* he hurt, just so he was hurting *somebody*.'

Fredericks, happily, picked up the ball from there, saying, 'You say, "Whoever did it," George. But didn't Walter Stoddard do it?'

Bartholomew hadn't expected to be the center of attention, and his kleptomaniac's heart was troubled by all the eyes focused on him. That made him even more rabbity and hesitant than usual, but at last he said, 'I'm really not satisfied in my mind that he did, no.'

'But he confessed,' Fredericks said.

'I don't know why he did that,' Bartholomew said slowly, 'but I just don't believe he went around arranging for people to have accidents. That just wouldn't be like Walter.'

I wished Fredericks would ask, at that point, who Bartholomew *could* see in that role, but Fredericks decided to take another tack, and at least for the moment I thought it best to lie back and be simply a part of the herd, rather than do any overt questioning of my own.

The tack Fredericks took was to throw the question open to general discussion, saying, 'Does anybody else agree with George? Anybody else think Walter Stoddard isn't really guilty?'

'Of course he's guilty,' Rose Ackerson said irritably. 'He *said* he was guilty, didn't he?'

Molly Schweitzler made a small sound in her throat and suddenly looked very panicky, probably because of the harshness in Rose's voice, but Rose turned and patted her arm, murmuring at her to reassure her, and Molly settled down again, chewing, her expression vacant. I remembered how tough she'd been at the therapy session two days ago, and it was hard to think of this as the same woman.

Marilyn Nazarro called me back from contemplation of Molly again, saying, 'But he must be guilty, mustn't he? Why would anybody say they were guilty if they weren't?'

Beth Tracy, the sexual-hysteric, said, 'Maybe he wants to be punished for something else he did. There's a lot of that around, you know.' As though she were talking of the flu.

Fredericks jumped again. 'That's interesting, Beth. Is that what you think happened? Do you think Walter's innocent, too?'

'I don't know,' she said. 'I really haven't thought about it at all. But I guess he must have done it, mustn't he?'

Bob Gale jumped aboard, saying, 'Why? You just said maybe he confessed because he wants to be punished for something else, and now you say you think he's guilty.'

'Well, I don't know,' she said irritably. 'The police believe him, don't they?' She turned to me, bringing the whole thing unfortunately full circle. 'What do you think, Mr. Tobin?'

I hesitated, but there was nothing to be gained by lying, and maybe something to be gained by telling the truth, so I said, 'I think he's innocent.'

That wasn't the answer she'd expected. Since I was sitting right beside her she had to half-turn in her seat to get a really good look at me, which she did. She said, 'Why do you say that?'

I could only watch one person at a time, and now the obvious one for me to watch was Beth Tracy. I hoped Fredericks and Bob Gale were watching some of the others. I said, 'Because the guilty person left me a note saying so.'

She gaped at me. I made a fast – trying for the appearance of casualness – turn of the head, to see everybody but Molly Schweitzler looking at me, the same look of astonishment on every face. George Bartholomew, next to me on the other side, said, 'Did you show it to the police?'

'Not yet,' I told him.

Marilyn Nazarro, across the table, said, 'Why not? If you have proof that Walter Stoddard is innocent, shouldn't you give it to the police?'

I turned to her and said, 'I know Stoddard didn't do it, and I can prove it. I also know who did do it, but I can't prove it. I'm hoping that person—'

Beth Tracy exclaimed, 'You *know* who it is?'

I didn't, but it seemed like a worthwhile bluff to try. I told Beth, 'It's one of the people in this room. But I can't prove which one, so if I go to the police they'll have to come back and question everybody, search everybody's room, maybe be tough with people again the way they were before. There's only one guilty person in this room, but if I can't prove what I know to the police they'll have to treat all seven people here as though they might be guilty.'

'You're making all that up,' Rose Ackerson snapped. 'It doesn't make any sense, and you know it.'

I turned around again, to meet Rose's angry glare. 'What do you mean, it doesn't make sense?'

'If you know so much,' she said, 'why *not* go to the police? Tell them, "I know it's this person or that person, but I can't prove it." But if you know it why can't you prove it?'

'Knowing and proving aren't always the same thing,' I said. 'I was hoping I could convince the guilty person to go to the police' – I was stuck for a second, not knowing whether to say 'himself' or 'herself', and paused lamely, then went on – 'and make a full confession without having to be forced into it.'

Rose gave me a look of angry scorn. 'Now, why would anybody do that?'

'Because the only thing that will happen to the guilty party,' I said, 'is that he or she,' solving it that way, 'will get sent back to the place he just got out of. The guilty party won't go to jail or the electric chair or anything like that.'

'Just back to the asylum,' Rose said savagely. 'Oh, that isn't bad at all, is it?'

'It's better than being dead,' I told her. 'Like Dewey.' And had the satisfaction of seeing her eyes slip from mine for just a second.

But then she was back, as strong as ever. 'Oh, this is just talk,' she said. 'If you know all there is to know, just say to the police, "*That* one's guilty, put the pressure on *her* first. Or on *him* first. Let everybody else go until you're done with this one." Why couldn't you do it that way?'

'I could,' I said. 'I'd rather not, that's all.'

'I think you're just full of hot air,' she insisted, still pushing me. 'I don't believe you got any note, I don't believe you know anything. You're just fishing, that's all, talking mysterious and hoping somebody will fall over and say, "Oh, I did it! Oh, you

149

got me!'" But it isn't going to happen, because Walter Stoddard is guilty and that's all there is to it.'

She'd been getting louder and louder toward the end of that speech, and unnoticed beside her Molly Schweitzler's face had developed deepening alarm, until all at once she whimpered, a small but terrible sound, unnerving, not entirely human. It shocked all of us, and Rose forgot me at once, turning around to console Molly again, to pat her arms and murmur to her, and Molly's face gradually relaxed again.

I continued to stare at the two of them, baffled by Rose's manner. She was so belligerent, so angry, so determined that there should be no question about Walter Stoddard's guilt, and yet at the same time she kept challenging me to call in the police. Was she guilty, and defiant until the end? Was she afraid Molly was guilty? But in either case, her own guilt or her fear or suspicion of Molly's guilt, I should think she'd want to sit pat until she found out for sure whether or not I really knew as much as I claimed. If she were guilty she would have to know she *had* sent me the note, and how could she be sure I was lying about any other part of it? Unless there was some way for her to be absolutely sure I was bluffing, it made no sense for her to be the guilty one and at the same time challenging me. And how could she be sure?

'Mr. Tobin?'

Startled, I looked around, and saw everyone looking at me. The voice had been George Bartholomew's, and now I realized he'd been asking me a question, but I had no idea what the question was. I turned to him and said, 'I'm sorry, my mind was wandering. Would you repeat that, please?'

'I said, it seems to me if the guilty person was going to confess, they would have done it when Walter was led away. Once they decided to let somebody else pay for their crimes, I should think they'd be hardened to the kind of appeal you're trying to make. Don't you think so?'

I was afraid he was right, and said so, adding, 'I was just hoping for the best. I thought, in this situation, in the therapy session here, the guilty one might realize the truth was the best thing after all.'

Marilyn Nazarro said, 'Mr. Tobin, *are* you telling the truth?' She was sitting next to Rose Ackerson, who was devoting all her attention now to Molly, and in a way Marilyn had picked up Rose's fallen standard, except that she was carrying it in a far quieter and more civilized way.

I told her, 'I *did* get a note from the guilty person, who *is* one of the people in this room. I'll tell you that for a fact, I'll swear to it, and Doctor Fredericks will tell you I'm telling the truth. I don't want to say any more than that.'

They all turned to look at Fredericks, who said, 'It's true enough. Mr. Tobin just told you the true facts. I hadn't thought he was going to bring them out in the open like this, I'm not sure it was the wisest thing to do, but it is the truth.'

Donald Walburn abruptly muttered, 'They'll stick together, Marilyn, don't believe either of them. When you find people sticking together, they're always up to something to get somebody else. Believe me, I know.'

I didn't want us to get back into a discussion of Donald Walburn's paranoia again, and luckily neither did Doctor Fredericks, who said, 'Marilyn, what made you accept Walter's confession at face value?'

She was surprised by the question, but no one else filled the silence she left, so after half a minute she said, 'I don't know. I suppose I just took it for granted.'

'Because the police believed him.'

'Yes, of course.'

'But the police don't know Walter, and we do. Shouldn't our opinion supersede that of the police?'

Beth Tracy said, 'But they're specialists, aren't they? I mean, just like you're a specialist, so we believe you when you talk about psychiatry and things like that.'

The conversation spiraled slowly from that point, Fredericks and Beth and Marilyn turning the question of belief and knowledge and specialism around and around, and I settled back to think things out. I looked at the faces around me and compared them with the attitudes they'd been showing, compared the attitudes with the reality of the situation and the kind of crimes we'd been dealing with, and found myself slowly sinking into a morass of possible motivations and unlikely exposure methods, and just as I was about to give up in disgust I saw a glimmer of light. I saw a possible answer to a secondary question, and that led me to another answer, and then another answer, and all at once I saw the thing neat and clean and clear.

Now all that was left was to prove it.

TWENTY-FIVE

The hour was nearing its end, and nothing more of any value had happened. I'd bided my time, waiting for the right opportunity, and it came at last as a result of something Bob Gale said.

It was a speech he made, actually, a brief but impassioned speech about protecting ourselves, protecting our pride and self-respect from the ugly bluntness of the local police. This led directly to a split down the middle of the group, between those who agreed with Bob's estimation of the police, and those who thought the police excellent specialists who could be relied upon to do their job well, regardless of an occasional incident like the beating up of O'Hara and Merrivale – and hadn't O'Hara and Merrivale brought that on themselves in the first place? Bob and Beth Tracy and George Bartholomew were all on the side of believing the local police inefficient and brutal. Donald Walburn and Rose Ackerson and Marilyn Nazarro were of the opinion, in differing ways and for differing reasons, that the police were basically good and efficient. The debate waxed hot for a while, and both Fredericks and I let it go, since impassioned people sometimes say more than they intend. But when I judged the peak of the argument had been passd I took the first handy pause in which to say, 'We haven't heard from Molly yet. What do you think of the police, Molly?'

She responded to her name by looking at me, but she didn't respond to the question at all. Her expression was mostly blank, with vague worry overlapping it like a thin cloud layer.

I said, 'What do you think, Molly?'

Rose Ackerson said, 'Leave her alone. She doesn't feel like talking today.'

'But you were doing so well the other day, Molly,' I said. 'You'd decided you weren't going to take any more cruelty from anybody, remember? You were going to fight back at last. No more overeating, no more self-pity, you were going to fight back. Remember saying that?'

The look of worry was growing less vague. 'I don't want to talk today,' she said. Her voice was frailer, more childlike, than it had been before.

'I can understand that, Molly,' I said. 'Maybe you can get

Rose to write a note for you, if you don't feel like doing your own talking.'

Rose snapped, 'What are you trying to do? We're in front of witnesses, you know, there is such a thing as libel. You'd better be careful what you say.'

I looked at Rose, and said, 'You kept challenging me to prove that I knew who the guilty one was, and that confused me. Unless you could be completely sure I was bluffing, you couldn't be guilty and want to challenge me. And how could you be completely sure I was bluffing?'

'Just from looking at you,' she said, angry and sneering. 'A man who's been a failure and a four-flusher at everything all his life, what else would you know how to do but bluff?'

'That's a good reason,' I said, 'but not good enough to make you completely sure of yourself. But I suddenly remembered something I'd said, about one person out of the seven in this room being guilty, and then I realized what the truth had to be.'

She pointed a trembling finger at me, trembling not from fear but from barely restrained rage. 'I've warned you about libel. I'm not going to warn you again.'

'The truth,' I insisted, 'is that *two* people were guilty, and if I didn't know that, obviously I didn't know anything. That table that collapsed on you two was *not* a rigged accident. It was the first of the accidents, and it caused the others, but it was not—'

'I'll have you in jail!' Rose shrieked. She was on her feet, and if Molly hadn't been sitting there helpless, Rose would have stalked from the room. But she couldn't leave Molly behind. 'You can't *say* these terrible things!'

'I can and I will. When that table collapsed on you two and everybody laughed, you both hated them. Molly hated everybody here, because they had laughed, and they became for her everybody in her whole life who had ever laughed at her and got away with it. And you hated them for what they'd done to Molly. Not because they laughed at you, you're too strong and self-sufficient to be affected by something like that, but because they laughed at *Molly*.'

'I suppose you and Walter Stoddard have some sort of homosexual relationship,' she said, trying now to switch to the haughtily superior. 'It shouldn't be hard for the police to get to the bottom of all this.'

'No, it shouldn't. I know Molly insisted on that note to me when I broke my arm, because after all I hadn't been here when everybody laughed, I wasn't one of the laughers and therefore I shouldn't be punished, and I know you wrote the note, just as I know she insisted on the note about Walter Stoddard being innocent and you wrote that one, but other than that I don't know which of you is responsible for what. I don't know which of you first suggested that you give other people accidents and see how they'd laugh about *that*, but it doesn't really matter, does it? You did it all together, one doing the sabotage and the other standing watch. As Donald Walburn said, when people stick together they're up to something. And what you two were up to was paying the whole world back for the lifetime of indignities Molly had suffered.'

'Who would believe such foolishness?' she demanded, but as she looked angrily around the table I saw her face change. I didn't look away from her, but I could guess the expressions she was seeing on the faces around her, and they wouldn't be encouraging, because this *was* the truth, and it had the feel of truth at last, and people can tell when things have the feel of truth.

I said, 'Molly.'

'Leave her alone!'

Fredericks said, in a voice so shockingly soft it was worse than any yell, 'Rose, sit down. Be quiet.'

'Molly,' I said.

She looked at me, reluctant, wary, childlike.

I said, 'Molly, Frank DeWitt never laughed at you.'

Rose was saying nothing now, but she was still on her feet, and she closed a hand tight on Molly's shoulder. I saw the touch stiffen Molly, and she slowly shook her head and said, 'We didn't do any of it. We wouldn't do things like that.'

I didn't know what to say next, how to reach her, and while I was still trying to think, George Bartholomew said, 'Molly, I never laughed at you. Don't you remember? When that table went over, I was right at the next table, and I jumped right up and brushed that coffee off your lap with my napkin. Don't you remember that? I never laughed at you, Molly, and look.' His hand, a thin hand with rabbity movements, went up to touch his cheek. 'Look what you did to my face,' he said.

'Oh,' Molly said, more a groan than a word, and her face crumpled, and she dropped her head forward onto folded arms.

Her shoulders looked huge, and they shook with sobs, and through the crying, muffled by her arms, we still could hear what she was saying, over and over:

'I'm sorry. I'm sorry. I'm sorry.'

TWENTY-SIX

Wednesday, the second of July. No humidity, no rain, no hovering clouds, only a high beautiful blue sky, a warm sun and a pleasant breeze. I was alone in the house, having called Kate when I'd come home from Kendrick last Friday and told her that she and Bill should stay at least a full month out there on Long Island. Of course I'd be all right, I told her, and she finally agreed.

Yesterday the doctor gave me a smaller cast, leaving both my elbow and wrist free, so that now I could keep my arm in a sling and even wear normal clothing instead of being limited to pajama tops. The itching was still fierce, but that was supposed to be a good sign. At least, they said it was.

The explanations with Captain Yoncker had lasted most of last Thursday afternoon and evening, so I hadn't been able to leave until the afternoon train on Friday. But they'd taken an affidavit from me, which would do in lieu of my presence at the inquest, and when I did leave Kendrick it was for good.

Rose had gone on denying the truth for nearly an hour after Molly'd broken down, and then she too confessed. Each woman tried to claim the lion's share of the blame for herself, but the official attitude was to apportion it evenly. Both would wind up back in asylums, probably for good.

The house had been fine to come home to, silent and restful after the pain and suffering of The Midway, but hampered by my bad arm I'd been unable to do much of anything and I'd been getting restless and edgy. I half-wanted to call Kate and ask her to come in for a day or two, but I knew she would react by calling off the vacation entirely, so I stayed away from the phone. I watched television, read, and had obscure uncomfortable dreams about the residents of The Midway, people who were fading more quickly from my waking mind than my sleeping mind. The weather was changeable all weekend, and then on Tuesday I got the smaller cast, and Wednesday was a beautiful day, and I stood on the back porch looking at my wall.

I hadn't worked on it for quite a while. It would fill the time, the way it always did, but here was my blasted right arm, useless, I didn't dare try to work with it, that would only delay the time when it would be healed and useful again.

One-handed? I looked out at the wall, inching up out of the ground all the way around my back yard, two feet thick, an unbroken line for three sides, with the house forming the fourth wall. I wouldn't be able to dig one-handed, of course, but what about laying bricks? It would be slower, but I cared nothing about speed, I had no deadlines to meet. All I had to do was one step at a time, all left-handed. It was at least worth a try.

And it worked. I got into old clothes and went out in the yard and the only difficult part really was preparing the mortar, but once that was done the rest was almost easy. Pick up the trowel, put down the trowel. Pick up a brick, put down the brick. Pick up the trowel, put down the trowel. Pick up a brick, put down the brick. The sun was warm, the air was fresh, the bricks were a beautiful color in the sunlight.

I'd sleep without dreams tonight.

There is an extensive list of NO EXIT PRESS crime titles to choose from. All the books can be obtained from Oldcastle Books Ltd, 18 Coleswood Road, Harpenden, Herts AL5 1EQ by sending a cheque/P.O. (or quoting your credit card number and expiry date) for the appropriate amount + 10% as a contribution to Postage & Packing.

Alternatively, you can send for FREE details of the NO EXIT PRESS CRIME BOOK CLUB, which includes many special offers on NO EXIT PRESS titles and full information on forthcoming books. Please write clearly stating your full name and address.

NO EXIT PRESS Vintage Crime

Halo in Blood — Howard Browne £3.99 pb, £9.95 hb
Halo for Satan — Howard Browne £3.99 pb, £9.95 hb
Seven Slayers — Paul Cain £3.99 pb, £9.95 hb
Fast One — Paul Cain £4.95 pb, £9.95 hb
The Dead Don't Care — Jonathan Latimer £3.95 pb, £9.95 hb
The Lady in the Morgue — Jonathan Latimer £3.99 pb, £9.95 hb
Murder in the Madhouse — Jonathan Latimer £3.99 pb, £9.95 hb
Headed for a Hearse — Jonathan Latimer £3.99 pb, £9.95 hb
Red Gardenias — Jonathan Latimer £3.99 pb

Green Ice — Raoul Whitfield £3.99 pb, £9.95 hb
Death in a Bowl — Raoul Whitfield £3.99 pb, £9.95 hb
The Virgin Kills — Raoul Whitfield £3.99 pb, £9.95 hb

NO EXIT PRESS Contemporary Crime

Hard Trade — Arthur Lyons £2.99 pb
The Killing Floor — Arthur Lyons £2.99 pb
Day of the Ram — William Campbell Gault £2.99 pb
Three with a Bullet — Arthur Lyons £2.99 pb
Ask the Right Question — Michael Z. Lewin £2.99 pb
Out of Time — Michael Z. Lewin £2.99 pb
Castles Burning — Arthur Lyons £2.99 pb (5/89)
Dead Ringer — Arthur Lyons £2.99 pb (5/89)
Act of Fear — Michael Collins £2.99 pb (6/89)

HARD TRADE — Arthur Lyons £2.99pb
LA's most renowned detective, Jacob Asch is on the street once more in a startling tale of Californian political corruption. A troubled woman hires Asch to uncover the truth about the man she is to marry. When Asch discovers the man is gay and the woman is run down on her way to a hastily called meeting with Asch, it becomes clear something big is at stake. Serious money real estate schemes, the seamy side of LA gay life and a murder frame involve Asch in a major political scandal that costs him his licence and nearly his life.

THE KILLING FLOOR — Arthur Lyons £2.99pb
David Fein, owner of Supreme Packing, a slaughterhouse in a grimy little Californian town had a problem . . . he was a compulsive gambler. First he couldn't cover his losses from the takings so he got a loan and went into debt. By the time he took in Tortorello, a clean cut Harvard type but with 'Family' connections he was in big trouble. Now he had been missing for 4 days and his wife was frantic. Jake Bloom, old family friend puts her in touch with Jacob Asch, who figures Fein is on a bender or in the sack with another woman — he's heard and seen it all before. But that's before he finds a body on the killing floor.

DEAD RINGER — Arthur Lyons £2.99 (available 5/89)
Jacob Asch is called in by boxing promoter Jack Schwartz to help out Carlos Realango, a South American heavyweight whose career is on the skids. He has been receiving threatening phone calls and Susan Mezzano his manager and mistress thinks her husband is responsible. Asch shows them how to tap their own phone and leaves it at that. Two weeks later Asch is called to Reno to prevent Realango tearing the husband apart only to find it is too late as Realango has been shot at Moonfire ranch, a fancy brothel, owned by the husband. The police say justifiable homicide, but Asch smells murder and something more than a lovers' quarrel.
"Lyons belongs up there with . . . Ross Macdonald" New York Times.

THE LADY IN THE CAR WITH GLASSES AND A GUN —
Sebastian Japrisot £2.99

Dany Longo is 26, blonde, beautiful and short-sighted. After borrowing her employer's car to drive to the south of France, she is confronted with one terrifying incident after another. She is handed the coat she forgot yesterday, the garage man checks the car he repaired the day before and a policeman asks her if she got back to Paris on time the previous night . . . when she had been there all day!

When she is attacked, her glasses smashed, her hand crushed and then she is confronted by a man in the boot of her car, Dany belives she is going mad. Japrisot brilliantly developes this into a tangled mystery story that won 'Le Prix d'Honneur' when first published.

NO EXIT CRIME CUTS brings the very best in crime writing, old and new at unbeatably low prices!

FAST ONE — Paul Cain (New Edition) £1.99

WAX APPLE — Tucker Coe (aka Donald Westlake) £1.99

Mitch Tobin, ex NYPD policeman was sacked for neglect that resulted in the death of his partner and friend. Racked by guilt, Tobin retires into a grim artificial world of his own until he is drawn out to investigate a series of suspicious fatal accidents at the Midway sanatorium. Five minutes after arriving Tobin is a victim himself, left with a broken arm, a headache and no idea where to begin. Then the fire escape collapses and the dirty game becomes murder!

LITTLE CAESAR — W. R. Burnett £1.99

CHICAGO. Girls and pimps, bootleggers and booze, killers and 'typewriters'. Go down the mean dark streets and see the cats sniffing the corpes. Go down the alleys and meet Rico, and Otero, Bat Carillo and Baa Baa Otavio, Killer Pepi and Kidney Bean. There are the squirrels, flapping to stay alive – Blondy Belle and Seal-Skin, Blue Jay and Olga. All playing for power. All certain to die! Little Caesar is the prototype underworld novel that inspired a whole generation of gangster films.

BURGLARS CAN'T BE CHOOSERS — Lawrence Block £1.99

Introducing Bernie Rhodenbarr, New York City's prince of thieves – who really should have known better!

When the mysterious pear-shaped man with a lot of uncomfortably accurate information about Bernie and his career offered him 5 big ones to liberate a blue leather box – unopened – it would have been a good time to plead a previous engagement, but times were tough. Everything was straightforward until two men in blue coats arrived before the liberation. Still all was not lost, there was always a way to work things out – but then they discover the body in the bedroom!